Look For Other Books By Linda J Pifer

Ohio Girl

A memoir of childhood and family in Ohio;
Stories of the Pifer/Guerin/Green/Wanamakers
and more; Illus. 92 vintage pictures, 122 pg.
Available on the author's' website.

Windows
Book One in the Windows Trilogy
An American widow begins her genealogic
research for the Smith Family at their country
manor in Yorkshire and becomes forever-
entwined in the family's history. 310 pg.

Daniel Smith – New Zealand Passage
Book Two in the Windows Trilogy
Travel with Daniel, the family's fifth-removed
grandfather as he sails to New Zealand's South
Island in 1847 for a new beginning which will
change his life and family history forever. 358 pg.

Visit the author's website at:

http://www.lindajpiferauthor.com

Copper Swift

Back to Highbridge

Book Three of the Windows Trilogy

Linda J Pifer

Cover design by Linda J Pifer

Photograph Aberdeen Ardoe House Hotel & Spa,

courtesy of Mercure Hotels©

Published by Readingseat Books

An LLC Company – U.S.

Available from Amazon.com

and other book stores.

ISBN: 978-0-9890142-5-0

First Edition

DEDICATION

To Family~

Yours and Mine,

Bless them

Wherever they may be...*Linda*

CONTENTS

Chapter One – The Copper Swift Mill

"Highbridge Estate is slowly failing; with the Copper Swift Mill completed we might have a chance..."

Dad's words echo inside my head as I enter the Mill's site office.

"Morning," I call to our engineer at his desk.

"Thomas," he says, but stays focused on his work.

I'm drawn to the window to look out at the land. It's mid-June across North Yorkshire; morning mists lift to reveal our two-hundred fifty acre Estate and the nearly-finished Mill on the Copper Swift River. *All hope is pinned on this;* the words repeat inside me and I can't forget, as heir to the Estate, how people depend upon our Smith family. I allow my head to drop in a silent prayer then straighten up.

Sarah lingers on my mind as usual. She still hesitates to set a date for our wedding though she captured my heart in 2010. I turn from the window and note that Joe's unusually quiet over the blueprints, his cup of coffee untouched. "Are you okay?" I ask.

"Maybe," he answers, "but there's something you should see."

"What are you looking at?" I join him at the table.

"I've been going over details before the Building Council's final inspection." He leans back to give me viewing space.

"Compare this elevation with the one on this page," he says and I pull the prints closer to take a look.

"Whoa, there's a difference here...over thirty centimeters on the walls!" Too flustered to say more, I compare the pages again.

"This drawing is flawed; why didn't we notice?"

"I don't know..." he rubs his forehead, "neither the foreman nor his crew caught it either, which is amazing to me.

"In truth Thomas, I should have been on top of this; it's my job and I take full responsibility."

"Too late for blame," I tell him. "We have to find a way to fix this before we risk final inspection...and I hope it won't be too costly because we're at the top of the budget right now."

Unable to say more, I head to the door then manage a half smile in his direction.

"I'm going down to do some measurements; you coming?" I want to throw something, but realise it won't help. I retrieve what's left of my self-control and promise myself a long run later this evening.

He joins me, "Do I still work here?"

"Right, I'll have to think about that..." I say in jest, but his face freezes and I take mercy on him.

"I'm aggravated with the whole situation Joe; of course you still work here." We walk outside and I hope for a miracle, a mistake on paper only.

The Mill is about a hundred metres walk down the gravel road. I study the building's roofline as we approach, but see nothing to hint at an error; the building itself looks amazing.

The whole idea was to make it appear old-school with modern materials and we've accomplished that. Its foundation is built with field stone from our land; the exterior, ordinarily of natural wood siding, is built with manmade siding, tough and durable. The roof appears to be metal, but it's actually 'sandwiched' panels with insulation and a lifetime warranty.

Copper Swift's noisy flow welcomes us as Joe and I climb up the front entry steps crafted of the same field stone. Their smooth, solid feel underfoot makes me appreciate the great job our local mason did. He executed the design perfectly and made the steps wide enough to accommodate several people at a time.

Stone posts around the edge of the veranda still await railings between them; the deck's surface is wet from the morning fog and deepened in color to reddish gold. This attractive outside space surrounds the building on three sides and with the small café' inside, our visitors should enjoy coming out to eat here when weather permits.

We enter to measure the wall to ceiling height on both floors then add in the floor's thickness. Our fears confirmed, the building's elevation is approximately thirty centimeters lower, thus the roof's edge as well.

"What's the impact on the water wheel?" I ask Joe.

"I'll look at the clearance requirements today, but that's not all; the prints will need reapproval if anything structural is changed and that could delay our opening date.

"Worst case Thomas, we might be ordered to remove some of the structure to correct the error versus working around it."

He faces me dead serious, "I don't know what to say except that I'll do all I can to make this right with a minimum of cost and time."

"I know you will, Joe and there's nothing more we can do until we get the facts. Give me the options when you have them, we can spare a few days to get the plan right before approaching the Council. Meanwhile, I'll brief Stephen on the situation."

"I don't know which task is harder, but I want to go with you to see Stephen, it's my responsibility," he says.

"Okay, but it's on both of us equally." I try to remain positive, but don't look forward to telling Dad either.

"Don't worry," I reassure him, "Stephen's a fair man and used to dealing with difficulty in business."

I decide to clear my head and walk up the hill to the manor rather than drive.

"You good with walking, Joe?" I ask.

"I'll drive and meet you there," he replies and turns to his car.

Copper Swift runs raucous, deep, tripping over rocks at its edges on its way south as I follow the gravel drive up to the manor.

As a ten year-old lad my days were filled with adventures on this river, especially after mum died. Dad lost himself in work but I waded and fished my way through my loss with the help of Emily, our housekeeper who tried to fill in where needed.

Did I ever think I'd build a mill along these banks at age thirty-four? The answer is certainly 'never', yet here I am.

Stephen and I both left Smith Imports in 2010 for two reasons; our family business founded over a hundred years ago had burdensome duties and long hours which kept us too much in London. Secondly, coming fulltime to the Estate has allowed us to address its pressing needs and shrinking finances while we still can.

As far as we know from Sarah's genealogic research I'm fourth generation at Highbridge. I've already made the decision to do whatever it takes to preserve our heritage for my own family someday, as my grandfathers did for me.

Chapter Two – Sneaking Around

I walk the damp grass through the back gardens to the Manor and shiver with anticipation. I've wisely picked a late night at midweek when everyone goes to bed early and smile with satisfaction.

An owl calls to his partner across the way and startles me for a second. Highbridge manor slumbers before me under a quarter-moon and the many windows in its four-storied wings are curtained against the night's cool air. Stone chimneys stand silent, except for one thin, pillar of smoke and all is quiet as I approach. *The risk doesn't outweigh my intent for the family* I think as I enter the kitchen then the back stairs, a secluded path to the darkened first floor.

I make my way across the oriental carpet in the formal dining room to stand shoeless at the main hallway.

Stay close to the wall, but avoid its many portraits. You don't need the sound of a heavy, sliding frame alerting the household to your presence at this hour, I think to myself. I keep alert, should anyone leave their room upstairs for a stroll to the kitchen and a midnight snack. I feel invisible dressed in black against this dark oak paneling, but think, *I've been almost invisible all my life.*

The manor's great room sits empty to my left, dark except for one of the two large fireplaces where dying embers still dimly light its wide hearth. I always marvel at the history displayed in there; three generations worth of portraits, swords, clan plaids and heavy furniture; all accumulated since distant Scottish grandparents built this manor with good Aberdeen granite. *So many ancestors on these walls and me with no one since mum and dad died years ago.*

At once a stranger stands just there; he stares into the embers with his hand upon the mantel, older and dressed from a past era. I freeze and lean back against the paneling, blink and look again, but he's gone and the room lies still.

A reflection from the mirrors on the wall; *a trick of my eyes,* I reason and move on after a glance over my shoulder. *Besides, old house, old spirits.* I chuckle, a bit nervous knowing I shouldn't joke about the dead. Still, I don't fear them even if they should exist. In my fifty-three years, I've seen plenty while serving this house, but never spirits at large.

Just past the library, I stop to raise the brass handle of the door into the coat room which lies tucked beneath the main stairs. Missy the house cat spots me with a meow and comes to stroke my trouser leg. I pet her once then send her off with a rude push of my foot. She takes the hint and returns to her nightly rounds. I can't take a chance at flipping on lights so enter with a flashlight and close the small door behind me.

I take a deep breath then whisper *"Where?"* and shine a sweep of light around the room. The family's genealogist, Miss Sarah, discovered the secret space behind the library shelves last year, just on the other side of this wall. It contained many old documents, pieces of jewelry belonging to Stephen Smith's mother and a brass letter seal with a shell imprint. In doing so, she unwittingly provided me inspiration to continue my nighttime searches.

Years ago as a growing lad in the village, Highbridge became a hobby for me based upon rumors of serious treasure existing here. Now, after overhearing the family's ownership of the Estate is in jeopardy, I've put away a child's excitement at discovering 'treasure' and made it my mission to do a thorough job of my search.

The seriousness of my actions is not lost to me, and my intrusion into the family's privacy wouldn't be taken lightly if discovered. Consequences could include loss of reputation, my job and standing in the village, perhaps even my freedom. Time has been on my side, chance has provided me opportunity, but now something inside me dictates there can be no going-back and I continue my searches with more urgency.

I turn the flashlight to the room's dark paneling on my right and trace the joint seams with a fingertip, but there's no palpable difference between the panels to indicate a secret door. The baseboard shows no irregularities, its thick oak runs from corner to corner without break and the floor's patina is undisturbed by rub marks to indicate a moving panel; likewise the front and back walls render the same results.

Undiscouraged, I turn to the fourth wall at the back of the stairs but it's completely concealed behind the long coat rod which spans the room's full width and is packed solid with coats and seasonal paraphernalia. Behind the hanging coats are tons of boxes, some in the front row labeled 'Extra wellies' and 'Serving ware'; lord knows what the boxes behind hold. Fox hunts were held on the Estate for decades and even folding chairs for their hunt boards are stacked here.

Pulling all this out will take work, but judging from the amount of dust, nothing has been moved in decades and it's just the sort of place that may yield a few interesting secrets.

It's an hour before dawn now and I need to vacate before Mrs. Courson, the head housekeeper, starts her morning rounds. I'll return to move more boxes and allow at least four hours to unpack and replace everything as it was.

What a bunch of pack-rats I think and open the door to look up the hall before leaving. In doing so, my leg brushes a large basket of brollies beside the doorway and they tip precariously off-balance. I grab the entire thing just in time to keep it from falling.

Footsteps down the hall prompt me to draw back inside until I hear the sound of the front door open and close.

After a few minutes I take a chance and look to see the hallway clear. Jamie, the house chef may already be at work in the kitchen so I make a hasty exit back the way I came to the dining room and leave through its terrace door.

Chapter Three – Problems

"ood morning Sarah." The shop owner's son waves to me and holds the door open for a customer.

"Stop by when you have a chance so we can catch up, Cheers," he adds and I wave back before he disappears inside his father's antiques shop.

He's been a friend since he helped identify the war medals I found in Highbridge's attic last year. His later discovery of a secret drawer in the old desk he restored for us was mind-blowing. Its contents included a very large gold nugget, a native-carved jade talisman and an old colt pistol; important clues hinting at Smith family history connected to New Zealand.

The village is busy for a Monday morning I note and keep a brisk pace while I enjoy its store windows on my way home. Though small, the village offers a market, a combined ice cream parlor and bakery, a chemist, a book store and the antiques shop. I use the local market because it's close by and helps me keep my new year's promise to walk more. Being able to meet some of my new neighbors at the same time is an unexpected benefit.

With today's lovely weather and blue sky overhead, I'm thankful the lane to my little cottage is dry and easy to travel on foot. I was relegated to the car last week after rain filled up the ruts.

This new lifestyle in the U.K. has been challenging and I know I'm not in Florida anymore. One of the hardest changes is driving on the left and I struggle to make the crossover from my U.S. driving habits.

The purchase of a shopping trolley to roll my groceries back home was necessity, but I smile when I think what mom would probably say; 'Sarah Sandlin, you're just thirty years old and a 'trolley lady.'; shopping carts seem to indicate senior citizen status back in the States.

I'm pretty sure Mom's a little antsy to hear a wedding announcement from Thomas and me but it's only been eight months. With that said, it does sound a little lengthier than I'd originally intended. I pause at the thought, but rather than think about it now I notice the bookstore's 'Open' sign is out and stop in to see the owner who ordered a case of my books last week.

"The shipment came over the weekend," she tells me, "and it's first thing on my list for today; I should have them in the window by this afternoon."

"That's wonderful; I appreciate your business and can't wait to see them on display," I tell her. "I wrote 'Genealogy 101' years ago, but my customers here have asked for it. It was about time to bring it up to today's technology anyway and get it back out there, so I hope they like it."

"I've already read it and I know they will," she says with a smile. "I'm serious about a signing when you get ready; let me know a potential date and I'll arrange it."

"Thanks so much, I'll do that. Have a great day."

"You too," she says and I continue the trek home.

Word is beginning to spread about my genealogy research business out of my cottage. Stephen has been more than gracious in allowing me to use him as a reference and three local families hired me to delve into their family histories. The Smith history is progressing well and we're very close to more info about Daniel Smith, their fifth-removed grandfather.

Sparrows hop in and out along the fence; roused from searching for choice bugs, they fly off to return after I pass. Wild garlic grows along here and several stalks of purple foxglove stand at attention near the lane's end. It's wonderful how nature provides its own landscaping with wild flowers since I've never had much luck as a gardener.

The combination of hills and green fields full of sheep make a beautiful backdrop for my new cottage. Sometimes I bring my morning coffee out to the back deck just to enjoy this new 'kingdom'. Life in North Yorkshire is quite different for me; in Florida the high humidity and temperatures often kept me in the house. Though it rains more often here, the cooler temperatures suit me fine.

Straight in the front door and through to the kitchen, I begin to put away groceries, but hear a car drive in. It's Thomas I see through the window and I open the kitchen door to him.

"Well Mr. Smith, this is a welcome surprise. You're usually stuck at your desk by now," I call to him as he walks from his car.

"I needed to get away and see you," he says and reaches to take me in his arms.

"Ah, this is what I've needed." He holds me close then adds, "I love it here."

"Me-too," I answer, quite content to stay a few moments here. Between his work on the Mill and my business, time together has been sparse of late.

"Anything wrong?" I ask. He draws back to look at me.

"Good observation—the word 'wrong' fits my condition; in fact, you're the only high spot in the day so far." He leaves me to help himself to a biscuit from the table.

"Heavens, that doesn't sound good; would you like some coffee with that?" He nods and we take our cups to the living room where the small sofa and light from the six pane windows invites us to relax. The gas fireplace has done a good job at taking the chill off I note; Thom soon exhales as he sits beside me.

"Joe found an error in the blueprints this morning," he tells me. "It may cost us more money than we have to correct it."

"Oh, no; what happened?" I ask.

"There's a variance in the height of the walls; the clearance requirements for the water wheel may be affected. Long story short, if we can't correct it, we'll have to postpone the opening. Our budget was tight from the beginning..." He fades off without finishing.

"Oh Thom, I'm so sorry. When will you know something for sure?"

"Joe's meeting with another engineer in the morning; he'll bring the options to Dad and me afterward. The thing is, I don't know Dad's resources since we left Smith Imports last year. He's been close-mouthed about his personal monies as usual and I don't feel I have the right to ask."

He begins to pace the room and adds, "I have some savings of course, but they could be a drop in the proverbial bucket. This project is a big part of our effort to bolster the Estate's finances and the worst of it is the waste. If we can't finish what we've started, it'll be a huge disappointment to the farmers in this area. They're depending on us to succeed and stimulate new commerce."

The pressure on him must be tremendous I think and try to somehow encourage him.

"Try to hold up until the facts are in, okay? I know it must be an enormous thing to ask, but it's all wasted effort before you know what you're dealing with."

"You're right of course Sarah, but it's hard to remain optimistic."

"There is something you haven't thought of." I muster up a smile.

"What's that?" he asks.

"You're not alone in this; your father believes in the Copper Swift Mill and so does mine. I'll bet there are others who'd be interested in buying shares to invest in the project. Don't feel you're holding the entire weight on your shoulders darling, you have a lot of people behind you and we'll find a way." I hope I've said something useful, but he walks away without response and stands at the window.

I feel I've failed which is not entirely new to me where Thomas is concerned. He's used to being independent in everything and it's difficult for him to accept help from anyone outside of his father. Though I'll shortly be his wife, right now I feel pretty 'outside'. I turn to the mantle and give it a swipe with my finger to make circles in its dust.

After a few minutes, his arms surround me from behind and he buries his face in my hair.

"How did you get so smart Sandlin?"

I turn around with a smile, "Guess I was born that way, Smith." He kisses me warmly and we draw close to each other. Time evaporates until my orange tiger cat comes stroking around our trouser legs and we both look down at him.

"Do you mind? You've interrupted time with my girl," Thom jokes.

"Okay." I return from my place on another planet to take advantage of the interruption. "I think Jamie must be preparing lunch right about now at Highbridge; shall we drive over and see what's on the menu?"

"Lunch together?" Thom asks, "That'd be great; you haven't been up to the Estate for weeks and everyone misses you, including me."

Well, that diversion was easy and proves the only thing more important to a man than necking with his fiancé is food; I can't help but smile and he sees.

"What?" he asks.

Stephen and his new wife Meg are just sitting down for lunch as we enter the kitchen, but he comes to welcome me.

After a few weeks away from Highbridge, I find myself amazed all over again at its size and this kitchen is no exception. The gray stone walls, white cabinets all the way down the inside wall and the light from the windows down its full length make it perfect for family meals; it's the one place I truly felt at home on my first visit last year. The Smiths get together over good food like any other family, never mind they go back hundreds of years and live on an estate.

"Sarah, what a nice surprise," Stephen says and after a hug, pulls out a chair for me. "We thought you'd disowned us."

"I'm sorry Stephen; and Meg, I know we had a tentative date to go shopping last week, but I'm really busy with the research business, thanks to recommendations from you both."

Meg smiles, "No problem Sarah, it's been the same here with the Mill's construction."

"Glad I could help," Stephen adds. "I know what a zealot you are when it comes to family history, but don't let it take over your entire life." He motions to Thom.

"No worries; I care too much about all of you to do that." I cast a look for his benefit in Thom's direction, too.

Jamie, the house chef, greets us from the counter and brings a platter of sliced ham and homemade rye bread to the table. Next are the fixings; a beautiful tossed salad and all sorts of add-ins including sweet pickles, a nice chutney, two different cheeses, mayo, hot mustard and crisps. I note a scrumptious-looking pie on the counter and groan at the sight; I won't be able to refuse that.

"Is that Blueberry pie?" I ask Jamie.

"Yes it is, Miss Sarah; strictly 'no-cal' though," he declares with a devilish, lying grin.

"Well in that case, reserve a small piece for me. Any whipped cream?" I ask as everyone laughs.

After lunch, Stephen pushes his plate back and focuses his attention on me. "I imagine Thomas told you about our little difficulty, my dear?"

Before I can answer, Thom drolly remarks, "Little difficulty" with a roll of his eyes.

"Yes 'little' in the scheme of things," Stephen tells him. "Granted, it's a disappointment and a setback, but there are very few endeavors in the world that don't suffer one or both of those; am I right?" He looks to Meg.

"Yes, dear," she speaks up, "you're entirely right and I would encourage you both not to get too depressed over this; things will work out."

Meg was Stephen's secretary at Smith Imports for years; she and Thom's mother Irene, planned the many parties and meetings held at Highbridge until Irene's sudden death of a heart attack in 1982.

When Stephen and Thom left the company last year, Meg was invited to come along and continue working as assistant for Highbridge Estate. It was a 'wonderful change' from the rush of city life she told me and she was thrilled with the little apartment for her on the third floor.

Out of mutual respect over so many years, something more began to flourish between them and last Christmas, he proposed. She accepted and they married in February. Meg, a widow of several years, has softened in appearance; her eyes have a sparkle that wasn't there before. Apparently country life and Stephen have agreed with this Londoner.

Thom picks up on Meg's advice; "In fact, a very wise lady told me much the same thing earlier today." He looks over at me. "Sarah came up with what I think is a brilliant idea to stretch our funds; would you like to tell them about it?"

"Yes," I reply and take a quick swallow of milk to clear my last bite of sandwich.

"I wonder if you've thought of how many people are on our side for this mill; the locals, your friends and family and mine. Should funds become a problem, perhaps you might think to sell shares in the Copper Swift Mill."

"Hmm," Stephen reflects. "A sound idea to be sure and I'll keep it in mind my dear. Honestly, I'd like to keep the Mill in the family if at all possible, but you're right; always good to have an alternate strategy should we find ourselves in dire straits."

Thom looks at me and I nod; it's enough for now.

"Jamie, have you seen Sarah today?" Emily asks as she enters my kitchen. Emily Courson has been chief housekeeper at Highbridge for decades and though I imagine she's somewhere in her fifties, she certainly rules the manor with a capable hand.

"She visited earlier for lunch," I reply, "but I believe she's left...although, check the library; she said she had a few things to look up before going back to her cottage."

"Thanks Jamie." She waves and walks out at her typical, no-nonsense pace; off to the library I suppose as I return to the after-lunch clean-up.

It's been said she looked after Mr. Thomas after his mother died. Her energy is amazing and I only hope I have some of the same at her age.

I finish up and take a break to plan the evening meal, but can't help thinking about the discussion during lunch.

My parents are very excited about the opportunities the Mill will offer; Dad raises wheat and oats and plans to join the Co-op with other farmers to sell grain to the Mill...what a shame if it doesn't open.

Stephen already has my respect for his influence on our community. He provided the low interest tuition loan for my chef school and as well to one of the Estate's garden crew to start an engine mechanics course last year. Other young people chose trades over the years with his encouragement and I know of at least six who've benefited from his financial assistance.

What Sarah said earlier is so true, this community is solidly behind the Smiths and I'll be there for them in any way I can.

I hope Miss Sarah is still about I think as I walk quickly upstairs to the library after speaking with Jamie. I need to talk with someone 'unofficially' and she's always been so friendly and down to earth.

Though she's lived in our country less than a year, she's earned everyone's admiration here at Highbridge and will someday be a partner for Thomas in running the Estate when it comes to him.

I think what a good match the two of them make, but I'm surprised they haven't set a date yet. Ah well, I remind myself as I reach the main hall; chief housekeeper I may be and they've all been just like family these many years, but the family's personal business is not mine.

I turn in at the doorway of the library to find Miss Sarah still looking through some old records and she looks up in surprise.

"Emily. Good to see you, how are you? Come in, we haven't had a chance to chat lately."

"Hello Miss, I'm just fine; hope I'm not interrupting you?" I ask, but come right to the point before she has a chance to reply.

"I just wondered if you've noticed anything unusual in the house during the last few weeks, Miss."

"Well...no, I haven't Em, but I haven't been here very often. Why do you ask?"

"I feel rather silly, but I think something's going on during the night." I can't keep my voice from shaking a little.

"Emily, are you alright? Come sit here and tell me what's wrong." I follow Miss Sarah to the chairs by the window.

"On several occasions now, there've been unusual sounds in the house."

"What kind of sounds?" she asks.

"It's hard to describe really; sometimes it's just a creak or a faint noise not heard before. My goodness, I've lived here for decades, but lately there are new sounds; nothing definite but still, unusual."

"Could it be an animal Em, maybe a mouse or a rat has entered through the chimneys."

"Well, it can't be ruled out that's certain. Maybe I should have an exterminator in for a good go-over; I hadn't thought about that before. Missy the cat has always taken good care of us, but she's getting on."

"Sounds like a good idea Em; talk to Stephen and get someone in."

"I will Miss and thank-you for helping me sort this out. I was beginning to think it might be an intruder."

"Em, I doubt the kinds of sounds you're describing are human, but have you asked the rest of the staff about unusual noises?"

"I've been too concerned that it's all in my mind, I guess. You know, keep up a strong front and all that; I do have my reputation." I manage a little smile.

"Yes Em," she says with understanding, "but no one could accuse you of not being brave and strong the way you've kept up this big house for so many years. If you ever need anything, I hope you know I'm always available?"

"I will Miss and thank-you. Now, I need to get on with my duties."

"See you later Ems," Miss Sarah says as I leave. I do feel much better.

Chapter Four – Working it Out

"We have to add another thirty centimeters to the walls, Thomas," Joe says calmly as we sit in the kitchen with our morning coffee to discuss his engineering consult.

My heart plummets to my feet with the news.

"It'll take heavy equipment to lift the roof and all would be closely monitored by the Building Council; they'd have to give their approval at every stage before signing off." I hear him and think of the potential variants; weather, cost of heavy equipment; my mind is going in circles.

"Thomas, you okay?" he asks and it dawns on me he stopped speaking a few minutes ago.

"Yeh, I'm good. I'm having trouble knowing where to begin that's all." After a deep breath, I take a stab at it.

"Call our contractor, bring him in and show him the problem in confidence, at least until we have a plan. Tell him we need a solid estimate on the cost and if he knows other alternatives, he should bring them along with corresponding costs."

"Got it, I'll phone him from the site-office," Joe answers. "You want to bring your father up to speed?"

"Yes, I'll do that now; see you later." I leave straight-on to find Dad.

I knock casually at the open doorway to Dad's private 'office' upstairs in the master suite. This large, high-ceilinged room never fails to remind me of my dear mother and was one of our favorite spots when we played hide and seek. The large Victorian bed with its carved newel posts and heavy spread provided a dark, spacious hiding place underneath for this ten year old on many occasions.

"Dad, do you have a moment?"

"Yes, of course, come in son, I'm just clearing up some bills." He's at the big desk in front of the windows and I take a seat near the fireplace where he joins me.

"I've just met with Joe after the consult this morning," I tell him. "It isn't good news I'm afraid; we'll need to add another thirty centimeters to the walls to meet code requirements."

"I see; not the news we wanted, but here it is." Worry shows on his face for a brief instant then he brightens to ask, "Well, what's next?"

"I'm not an expert on this, but Joe says perhaps the roof could be separated and lifted then reattached. It sounds very costly and I'll wait on our contractor's opinion before we consider it."

"Heavy equipment would be required I imagine?" he's already guessed the answer.

"Yes and because of the size of the Mill, I don't know what type. Joe is setting up a meeting with our contractor as we speak."

"Well then, I suggest we try to remain calm and get some input as soon as possible."

"I agree, and he'll handle it timely; any questions I can answer for you in the meantime?" Dad sits up straighter and I know his next question before it's asked.

"The obvious, son; how did this happen?"

"It was human error, a comedy in domino-like order; Joe and I figured it out yesterday. The draftsman made the error, but Joe and I missed the difference on page two of the final print.

"Page two is the construction drawing," I explain, "the page our contractors followed; they probably didn't notice because there's no visual flaw apparent on the building. But for the fact we need the extra space for the wheel on the back wall, it could go unnoticed and none the worse."

"So it was the draftsman's error?" Dad says.

"Yes, but we signed off on his work and there's no remediation open to us on that score; it's our problem now."

"Then we'll explore our options, pick the best solution and go on from here," Dad says.

He looks back to the papers on his desk and I feel deep regret at this setback and personally responsible, but I know he won't say further. He's never been one to hold a grudge, an attribute I'm very grateful for.

"I'll leave now if there's nothing else; see you at dinner." I attempt some levity, "I believe it's hamburger night, per Sarah."

"Well, good news for a change," His says with a subdued smile

By one a.m. I'm up the back stairs and on my way to the front closet again, the third visit this month to dig through junk stored there and more importantly, to see what lies in the deep space directly behind the stairs. It's taken longer than planned and I hope to finish it tonight.

So far I've met no one on my nighttime forays and have no intent to do so. The only near-disaster was the tipping of the brollies basket; whoever left by the front door that morning didn't seem to hear. It was a close call, actually the closest since my searches began.

When I began listening to gossip about Highbridge as a child, it was astounding what casual talk and hearsay could reveal. Everywhere here and there in the village, bits of info reached me via elderly relatives who talked about the old days, some even worked for the Smiths.

The first I heard of hidden treasure, I was a young lad of twelve and hung about our kitchen after school to watch Dad play chess with his cronies.

I suspect the old men used the game to escape their wives and chores but I was too young to realise it then. They arrived in threadbare, but clean attire; most wore heavy beards of different styles and covered their heads with worn-out hats to keep off the damp, cold weather.

Dad welcomed them weekly; my mum wasn't in favor, but she went mostly unheeded, as usual. A bottle brought down from the cabinet for a wee sip started every game and I suspect my father provided it at his expense, much to mum's chagrin.

Things were not good in the village in those days and jobs were few. Primarily a farming community, farmers did their own work with several sons beside them and extra help was hired only occasionally, during harvest time.

One day, a man talked about the 'old days' when his father was a young hire at the Estate, shortly after the Smiths moved in. He bragged on knowing their wealth was made in gold and his parents said some of the gold was hidden in the new house during its construction.

The man noticed me then and downplayed it all with a hearty chortle. He said his father was a bit balmy in his old age and actually stole furniture out of the house after the Estate's master became ill. It remained in my young mind despite his efforts otherwise and I started keeping a journal on things Highbridge then and there.

I made another entry a few years later when a great aunt, once a young housemaid, told my mum they'd had 'visitors' at the Estate from a faraway island. She 'accidentally' overheard talk of a gold mine being closed and a remark that the family's 'heirloom collection' would be preserved for the future. She described each point with a raised eyebrow, intimating it held great importance that I didn't understand then.

My reflections end as I lift the latch and slip inside the familiar closet. But immediately I feel *something isn't right here*...a dark shadow in the far corner catches my eye.

I look closer but the shadow changes from dark to light, suddenly bright enough to reveal a tall figure. An older man takes shape and I almost drop my flashlight...then notice its lens is dark...I haven't turned it on yet...but there's light all around me; *how can that be?*

I feel glued to the spot, fascinated, but shocked at the same time. A light mist lays around his feet as he stands silent a few steps away and the pit of my stomach tells me he's not part of this world.

The flashlight drops from my hand and I reach behind me for the door latch...slip out and close the door in case 'he' wants to follow.

I'm in the hallway where anyone can see me now and I realise the obvious; he probably could follow with little effort. It's unusually cold and I don't feel well, but try to remain calm and concentrate on reining in my imagination; it's not easy. If ever I were to see a ghost, the man in the closet meets all my expectations.

I attempt to talk myself down while keeping a wary eye up and down the hall; *you can't leave like this, you'll imagine all sorts of things if you walk away; get back in there and take another look.*

I place my hand on the latch, despite every shred of me resisting the move and slowly open the door.

The corner is empty and the coldness has left along with the uneasy feeling in my stomach. I walk into the corner but find no evidence that anyone or even the damp mist was ever here.

Alright, I acknowledge a little relieved at the spirit's absence; *one time is a reflection from a mirror, twice and in another location isn't my imagination.*

Thom is on my mind today more than usual as I busy myself about the cottage with some needed housekeeping; first target, the dust on that mantle.

Brian used to dust the house for me when I was busy writing; the thought of my first husband pops up unexpectedly. Though he'll always be part of me, the pain of his loss to cancer has faded. *It's been eleven years since his passing.* I think with pause.

When Thom's letter arrived last year to invite me to Highbridge it set off a soul-wrenching struggle in me to step outside the boundaries I'd built in grief. I had no idea then just how much his invitation would change my life.

Thomas was unexpected; how easily he disturbed the shell around my heart within three weeks of my arrival, I think with a smile.

I knew he was meant to be something more, but I went to extreme measures to deny it and returned to the States before I finally admitted it to myself.

When I returned here during the holidays, he proposed on Christmas Eve and I said 'yes' with one condition; we'd wait for a while to set a date and remain independent of each other. He was upset and disappointed, but understood more as we talked.

I needed time to establish myself in this new country and to make sure we really knew one another well; we'd only known each other for eight weeks at the time and for me, it was just too soon.

Today marks my eighth month here; I've lived independently and have a developing success in a career of my choice, both very important to me.

Losing my first husband so suddenly taught me that I need an established life of my own because sometimes marriage doesn't assure couples will be together always. Whatever the cause, I never want to be left at loose ends again.

I've learned more about Thom in these past months and know he's fiercely independent when it comes to accepting input, i.e., mine. I'm independent as well, but need to know my husband will trust me as an equal partner in the future life we build together.

I suspect the death of his mother at an early age has something to do with his misconception of what women expect today. That and the fact that Stephen probably shares some outdated beliefs on a woman's place in marriage and has passed that on to his son.

We need to talk out my concerns and any he may have as well, though in the past he's gone a little defensive when we differ in opinion. I'll keep communications open until we both learn to talk things out together.

And yes, I think with a smile, *I want several children to bring lots of laughter back to Highbridge.* For my part, being totally independent was good for a while, but lonely and it's time to move life along again.

There, I've admitted it for the first time and I'm filled with butterflies at the thought. I want Thom all the way in my life, but this isn't the time to tell him with the difficulties at the Mill. It just wouldn't be fair to put more responsibility on him right now.

The grandfather clock slowly tic-tocks as I move past it to enter the hallway. I have three hours to finish up my search and I vow this will be the last night I spend in that dusty closet room.

On previous visits, I rearranged the boxes behind the coat rack, those opened, those still to open...and no ghostly image has reappeared. I've accepted that the spirit seen twice is interested in what I'm doing, else why would he appear only to me? Had he intended harm he could easily have done so by now.

Besides, I don't believe ghosts have power over us. I finish that thought with the caveat 'if they even exist', but know there is indeed a ghost following me and it can't be denied. The next time he appears, I'll forget my apprehension and try to look for clues to his identity.

With the floor of the closet space finally cleared, I have a path to the back wall and stoop to take a look at it under the hanging coats. Before crawling in, I notice heavy dust everywhere and can't imagine what my clothes will look like afterward.

I suddenly sneeze quite loudly and clamp a hand over my face in case another one occurs. How stupid of me – I forgot about my allergies.

In the midst of another sneeze, a cloud of dust rises from the space and I take a step backward as a familiar coldness sets in. Braced, I look at the now-familiar man in front of me. I can just make out a scar on his forehead. His face is kind, but I feel my resolve to override fear dwindling, that is until he points toward the path I've just cleared.

I take the hint and follow his direction after my flashlight turns to the stairway space deep in the closet. It disturbs me only slightly that I have not consciously moved the flashlight and it has a will of its own.

There under the stairwell's first step is an object the size of a cigar box and I slide into the space without further thought. I forget the ghost, intent upon the retrieval of whatever is back there.

When I finally get a grip on it, I find it's metal, similar to a common bank box and pull it toward me. It rattles loudly over the floor and I stop to listen in case anyone is nearby.

Within a split second there's a footstep, just inches above my head on the front stair. I turn off the flashlight and freeze in my current reclining position, the silence and the dust.

The moment is interminable; I glance back and see the ghost has disappeared. *'Coward'* I joke to myself, but it's clear only I am meant to see that kindred spirit.

A second and a third step on the staircase signifies someone has reached the landing. My hand shakes, my nose itches, but I hold steady; shifting only slightly, I rest my elbow on the floor with the box still in hand.

The silence continues and I contemplate what could come next. The disarray of boxes stacked near the door will instantly appear out of place to whoever enters. With the thickness of coats packed onto the hanger rod, I doubt they'll discover me at first so I'll wait it out and stay here in my burrow.

In a few moments, I hear the door to the closet swing open and the words "Oh my!" I know immediately it's Mrs. Courson and hold my breath, expecting the worst.

But the door closes again and her quick steps down the hall tell me she's gone to the kitchen, probably to fetch Jamie since he's the only other person up this early. Without hesitation I crawl out with the tin box under my arm and look down the hall. The way is clear; I step out and with a split-second decision turn boldly towards the front door and leave.

I walk across the dark yard to my car as calmly as possible, never mind the fact I'm in my stocking feet and covered with dust. Luckily, I have my keys and start the car...just as someone taps on my window.

I manage to act as though nothing is amiss, take a deep breath and open the window with a smile for the Estate's gardener.

"Good morning John."

"Good day sir, gettin an early start I see," he remarks.

"Why yes, I have some errands to do."

"Well I won't keep ya then." He gives a little wave as he continues on to his work.

I exhale and take a moment to regain some composure until my heart beat slows a little. Then, with the tin box beside me, I drive the car slowly out the driveway.

Jamie called me from my room a few minutes ago, and asked that I join him in the front hallway; He said only, 'There's been a disturbance during the night, Mr. Thomas.'

"What's going on?" Stephen asks me as I arrive. "Jamie said something about an intruder?"

"Yes sir," Jamie answers from down the hallway and comes to meet us.

"Mrs. Courson came to the kitchen this morning to fetch me and was in quite a state. She'd come down the front stairs and heard something underneath the stairway. She's suspected a rat infestation and opened the coat closet to investigate."

He opens the coat room door for us saying, "Not exactly what she thought it was," then steps aside to show us.

"My word!" Stephen says and walks inside as far as possible, given the number of boxes everywhere. "Where did all these come from?"

"Dad, it's all been stashed behind the coats; remember the hunt club your parents used to host? These are extra supplies, even some taxidermy lurking in a couple of them, I believe."

"No wonder we have a rodent infestation," Dad declares.

"Except that we don't, sir," Jamie says. "The serviceman was here yesterday; he found no evidence of anything and said Missy continues to do her job."

"Well then, what is all this?"

"It may be the result of a larger 'varmint' Dad, perhaps human?" I pick up a flashlight on the floor to shine it under the coats.

"Whoever did this was very interested in getting to the back of the closet under the stairs and apparently made it." A clean path through the accumulated dust is no doubt being worn on someone's clothing at this point I think as Mrs. Courson comes around the doorway.

"Oh my..., she says and covers her mouth when she sees the dark path under the coats. "Someone might have been there when I first came in." Jamie puts an arm around her shoulders to steady her.

"Now Emily, we don't know that," I lie. We all know it could be true.

"Come on," I encourage her and take her elbow, "let's go into the library and get our stories together. Jamie, would you mind bringing a tray up for us? We could all use a little sustenance and some hot coffee."

"Yes sir, I'll have it up soon."

"Where's Berty?" Dad asks, "As our house man, I would think he'd be right here in this situation."

"He went into town to a dentist appointment sir, but should be back soon," Emily answers from my side. I soon have her comfortably seated in the library, with protest, of course.

"Oh Mr. Thomas, I can't sit here, I have chores to do."

"Now Emily, you've had a shock and I want you to sit still for a while and collect yourself, do you understand?"

"Yes sir, of course; I have to remember I'm not as young as I used to be."

"No Ems, you're not," I say in honesty, "but you're still the same woman you've always been and I don't know what we'd do without your talent for keeping us in order." She looks reassured and leans her head against the high-back chair. I take the opportunity to step out for a minute and let Meg know where Emily is.

"Dad, can I see you for a moment?" He follows me down the hallway.

"We have a thief about; should we notify the Constable?" I keep my voice low to prevent Emily from hearing.

"I believe you're right son. I'll make the call; you stay with Emily."

Constable Sheller took his initial report from Emily and Jamie then did a thorough inspection of the coat room.

A squared away, older fellow the Constable, with glasses he removes periodically to look at the person he's addressing. He asks little since we told him nothing is missing as far as we can see and he found no evidence of forced entry. He was a little shocked to hear that the kitchen door is usually left unlocked.

When his inspection is concluded, we follow him out to the front door.

"Anything else happening like this in the area?" Stephen asks.

"No sir," the Constable replies, "it's been very quiet. These things take some time to be worked out; I'll keep in touch. Meanwhile, if you notice anything missing or hear unusual sounds again, please give us a call right away.

"Oh, and I suggest you start to leave some lights on around here. Thieves are at home in the dark, at least make them nervous with more lighting at night." I notice a slight turn-up at the corner of his mouth after the advisement and he appears pleased with himself. He's taken the flashlight we found in the room for fingerprinting.

"You're entirely right Constable," Stephen tells him, "we'll do our part and thank-you for your quick response."

We return to the library and Meg joins us after convincing Emily to take a nap.

"Is she alright?" I ask.

"Yes Thomas, just badly frightened. A nap will do her good and I expect we'll see her down here to clean up that closet in a few hours, now that she's seen its dusty condition." We smile and agree it's probably true; she's known for keeping the house clean with a vengeance. I remember the attic when Sarah had us searching for genealogy clues last year. Poor Berty was put to task by Emily afterward for a giant cleanup.

"I'm disappointed this could happen at Highbridge," I remark to Dad. "It may be the first time anyone has tried to steal from us, do you agree?"

"Nothing of the sort during my time here, but father and mother found many of Grandfather's furnishings gone after he fell ill. Mother used to tour the sales on a regular basis and more than once returned with something she'd identified from the Estate."

"Illness provided opportunity to steal without attention," I suggest.

"Quite," Dad agrees, "I feel confident the Constable will investigate and keep an eye out for anything suspicious. Right now, we have nothing missing...this time."

"Yes, we've been fortunate but I want to heed the Constable's suggestion and rethink our security measures for the house and grounds. At the least, we need to leave some lights on in the house, maybe even install some motion detectors, and lock the kitchen at night."

"I'm not sure about motion detectors;" Dad frowns, "blamed devices always setting off no matter who's about...scared me half to death at a friend's estate one time. I came out to the kitchen for a snack and the whole place went off. Do you want to take this on Thom or hire someone in?"

"I'd feel better if we brought someone in; I'll find the right service on Monday and let you know. I also want some extra lighting outside and solar will save us money; John and his men can install it."

"Good idea, go ahead with it Thomas. I guess we're seeing a change in our world and it won't do to be fooled twice."

Meg senses his sadness, "Come dear, Jamie probably has lunch ready by now and we'll feel better after we eat."

"Quite right," he declares.

Chapter Five – Options

We take our seats in the library this morning to discuss options for the Mill's completion.

"Thomas, Mr. Smith," Joe greets me and Dad. "Let's get right to it if you don't mind? We all know Mr. Teppler, he's prepared some options, so Bill if you'll proceed..."

"Yes, I'd be glad to. Good morning to all of you; Stephen, it's been some time since we worked on a project together, I believe it was the garage, wasn't it?"

"It was and a good job, too," Dad replies.

"I'm happy you were pleased with it. Thomas, this is the first time I've seen you in many years; you'd just graduated university last time we met."

"Yes, it's been a while," I reply briefly, "many changes in my life since then. What can you tell us about the problem at hand, Bill? I'm eager to hear what we're up against."

"Well, as you've probably guessed, it isn't a simple fix and will require some work and additional expense.

"...didn't think we'd get off Scot-free," Stephen comments impatiently.

"I've prepared two options," Bill continues. "The first and most work-intensive would be to lift the roof in sections and add to the wall height all the way round." He shares a drawing of the project.

"It would take approximately five weeks at a cost of £38, 000," he adds.

We sit in silence as the cost and delay sink in.

"Is there any way to cut that down?" Dad asks.

"Unfortunately, the answer is 'no', Stephen. I've already eliminated large heavy equipment by doing it in sections vs lifting the entire roof; you don't want to hear expenses for that."

"Bill, you said you have two options; what's the second?" I ask hopefully.

"I actually think the second would be the way to go, Thomas, but of course the decision is yours." He hands out a second drawing which shows the waterside wall of the Mill with a redesign of the roof.

"As you can see, I've redrawn the roof to create a dormer of sorts with a line of insulated windows along its length; I believe it works well with the original design while giving us the height we need for the wheel's requirements. It saves our having to redo the entire wall and there's minimal roof work, beyond the buildout. You can imagine it will also give us additional light on that second floor which is never a bad idea. See what you think of it."

We examine the design quietly; I'm almost afraid to ask how much this will set us back.

Dad takes the initiative; "In the event we favor this design and can handle the expense, do you think the Council will approve it?"

"I've already met with one Council member unofficially," Bill tells us, "and he's more worried about the first option. He claims lifting the roof will require an entire new set of prints and approval; also it would make the building an "exception" to current standard. With this second option, we can submit an addendum to the plan and he feels it'll meet with approval."

I feel as if a light has broken through up ahead, but I'll reserve celebration until we hear the final word.

"Then give us the details on option two; we're anxious to hear," Dad encourages him.

"What I call, 'the eyebrow project', will also require five weeks, but at a cost of £20,000, it's by far the more prudent of the two. There's a chance we can finish sooner, if so, there'd be additional savings on labor, of course." Bill sits back to wait on comments and questions.

I look over at Dad and he's still studying the second drawing. Joe's smiling with relief at me and I return his nod.

"I'll sleep on this, if you don't mind Bill," Stephen says, "I want to be sure of our decision and that we can handle the additional time and expense."

"I understand sir; I'll wait to hear from you, say by the end of the week? As soon as I get the go-ahead, I'll have the plan of your choice drawn up and Joe can submit it for approval to the Council."

"Thank-you, Bill." Stephen rises to shake his hand then stays behind as Joe and I show him to the front door.

"Thanks again Bill, you don't know what a relief it is to find our way through this," I tell him.

"And I really like the 'eyebrow,'" Joe adds. "It's actually an improvement to the original design we hadn't thought of."

"Glad you both like it; good-day to you then."

We return to the library where Dad still sits studying the designs.

"The second design is the best, Stephen, in my opinion," Joe says. "And it's an improvement esthetically."

"I agree Dad; have you thought how the late afternoon sun will shine through those windows?"

He puts down the drawing without enthusiasm and remains quiet.

"Dad, what's going on?"

"Joe, would you excuse us; I need to speak with my son."

"Of course, see you at the office later Thomas?"

"I'll be down directly." I take a seat at the table with Dad.

"It's very hard for me to say this Thomas; I never thought we'd come to it."

"Dad, whatever it is, you know you can tell me."

"No father wants to tell his son that his inheritance is just about gone...but that's what I have to tell you now."

I sit back in shock; I can't say that I'm exactly surprised and have wondered for some time about our reserves. But, I didn't believe it would ever come to this.

"Define 'just about' Dad and please be clear."

"A few investments remain in the Estate's Trust fund; slow-growing but reliable; some bond-money and about £100,000 in liquid funds. Of course, my shares in Smith Imports are intact."

"I wondered about all this when we started the mill project, even asked you, but you confirmed our finances were in order; why didn't you tell me?" I ask then say more softly, "I would have continued working for the Company or somewhere else, to at least contribute." The last twelve months since we both left the family business in London run through my mind.

"A father wants to give his son and family what they're accustomed to and deserve," he answers. "I thought I could do this project, recoup the investment and begin to replenish the Estate's Trust fund.

"I still believe it's possible," he goes on, "but the lines are a little too close between red and black for comfort." He puts both hands down on the table, and seems unable to look at me.

"Then, this is not the time to give up Dad. The first thing to do is find a way to stabilize the 'bleed' of unnecessary payouts, starting with the Mill. I can afford to finish the roof project, this is something I believe in too; I'm a grown man so let me do this. It doesn't in any way diminish your position as the head of our family; it just means you trust me to do the right thing."

"Do you know how proud I am of you Thomas?" He asks and completely settles me down for a moment.

"I know, Dad; it's what drives me in life, knowing that very thing."

We've spent hours this week on the Estate's finances, discussing strategies and poring over the books. I feel comfortable we've covered all of it, the Trust's investments and remaining resources. We're writing it up now, with some improvement points to our investment methods. We both agree it needs formal documentation so we can refer to our goals in future.

"You have my permission to scout out any revenue changes you think wise, Thomas, including those for the Mill." Dad says as we work.

"Thanks for your trust; the shortage will be corrected to cover the Mill's debut," I tell him. "Additionally, I've set a goal of two years for the Mill to get profitable; should that not be accomplished, there's a possibility we'll need to sell some or all of your shares in Smith Imports, unpleasant to think of I know. Another option would be to go with Sarah's suggestion of selling shares in the Mill, instead." Surprisingly, he doesn't seem shocked at either suggestion and we arrange to meet with our banker next week.

Always at the back of my mind through all of this is my Sarah. Though the last few weeks' events have shaken me and my family, bringing her fully into my life has always been my number one priority. I see her as often as possible but there've been lengthy weeks between our visits lately.

The advent of contributing some of my assets to the Mill will have a direct impact on our lifestyle after marriage and even extras like our honeymoon will be a challenge; all lies heavy on my mind.

I understand now Dad's reluctance to tell me our financial problems and feel the same when it comes to telling Sarah about the family's present state of affairs.

It bothers me I'll be limited when it comes to providing for her. I don't want to see her under any duress in the future or feel she has to work to help support our family. It will be my responsibility as her husband to provide a good quality of life for her and she shouldn't have to expect anything but a serene, comfortable life such as my father gave mother.

One thing certain, we need to have a long talk as soon as possible. It should be in the clear light of day and I have an idea just where to do that.

"Sarah, good morning love." Thom's voice over the phone sounds a little unusual but I can't imagine why.

"Hello, what are you doing today?" I ask him.

"The usual, but I've been thinking; it is summer and we haven't been on a picnic yet. What do you say, a picnic tomorrow? I know a beautiful place not far from here."

"Oh Thom, I'd love to; where is it?"

"It's a surprise, but I know you'll like it. Wear some old clothes, hiking shoes and bring your bathing suit."

He teases me with scant details. "Very well, I'll let you keep your secret. What time?"

"Pick you up at the cottage around ten, if that's good for you?"

"I'll be ready, see you then – love you."

"Love you too my Sarah."

I hang up and wonder if this might be a good time to discuss things between us and let him in on my decision about the wedding. There's no way of knowing so I'll just watch for an opening and see what happens.

Thom arrives before ten this morning, but I'm ready.

"Good morning." He picks up my backpack and opens the car door for me.

We head east out of the lane and I remark, "Okay, we're rolling now Mr. Smith; where are we going?"

"Not yet; all I can say is your jeans and walking shoes are appropriate. Did you bring your suit?"

"Yes, but I can't imagine needing all these clothes and still going for a swim; I'm dying of curiosity here."

"Good, that was the general idea and it's working." He gloats with a sneaky grin.

"It's our road trip to Scotland all over again." I press my luck; "Will you at least tell me how long it'll take to get there?"

"Approximately thirty minutes." He turns the car onto another secondary road.

At about twenty minutes out, I see a sign that reads 'North York Moors National Park'.

"Aha!" I exclaim.

"Okay, I hear you celebrating over there; you think you've made a discovery, but you still don't know our destination." He gloats some more.

Five more minutes and we park at the end of some feeder road in the middle of nowhere. Don't get me wrong, it's a beautiful, green nowhere in gently, rolling hills divided by farmer's fences.

"Are you ready?" Thom asks.

"I remain positive here Smith, but it's becoming difficult; where are we?"

"We're here. Come on, I'll show you." He grins at me and comes around to open my door. I take his hand and he pulls me to him for a good morning kiss, sweet, sloppy and perfect in the sunshine. Then he leaves me in a partial daze to pull out our backpacks and an old blanket.

"Let's go," he announces.

"Go where?" I shade my eyes in the bright sun to look over the surrounding terrain.

"Follow me."

We hike through a farmer's field toward a bunch of trees and finally arrive at its edge. There's a pathway worn by someone or something, cows maybe and I follow him into the woods. Its trees are older growth, the floor under them thick with woody debris; various green plants grow out of a mossy carpet toward the meager sunlight that filters down. I'm reminded of some fairy-filled dale where any minute, little winged creatures will start flying around us.

"Sarah, are you coming along?"

"Yes, sorry." I reenter reality and keep up behind him.

In a moment the path breaks into an opening and I catch my breath at the beautiful lake laying still and green before us. We stand for a few moments to soak up the quiet until a magpie breaks into song.

"This is breath-taking," I say and drink in this little miracle place.

"I thought you'd like it. Let's find a good place for the blanket and our stuff, then we can take a swim, if you want," he suggests.

We spread out the blanket above the water's grassy edge and unload our backpacks on it.

"It's a work day so I doubt we'll see anyone else," Thom says. "People that live nearby know about this spot and bring their families on weekends, but it's a closely-kept secret. If you want to duck into the trees to change, I'll wait here until you finish."

I dip my toes in the water and it's surprisingly warm. "I'll do that," I answer, "this water is perfect."

When I return, he's already changed to his suit and raided the cookies in my backpack.

"The edge usually has some fallen leaf debris under the water," he explains, "so it's a little squishy, but it gets deep pretty quick." He offers his hand and we wade in. I see what he means about that first step; my foot sinks into dead leaves and mud but we both throw ourselves into the water ahead and swim free of it.

I come up from our dive laughing and push my hair back out of my face while Thom treads water beside me.

"I know nothing about lakes in this country," I tell him. "Back home we'd keep our eyes peeled for alligators. No danger of that here, I assume?"

He laughs and confirms "No danger."

"We also have water moccasins, cotton mouths and something called an amoeba which eats your brain if it gets into your nose or ears from the mud on the bottom."

"Good heavens," he exclaims, "are you sure you're from earth or some alien colony?"

"Quite sure Florida is on the earth," I continue, "when you grow up in it, it doesn't seem that freaky, but I guess to someone else, it might."

"You think?" he laughs. "Race you to the other side!" He's away before me and I follow close in his wake.

We sit on the other side of the lake to take a breather. "We do have a snake called an 'adder', Thom explains. "They're clay-white color with a distinctive, dark sort of 'ladder' design down their backs. They're poisonous but usually back off if you do the same and don't scare them."

"Oh that's comforting, but a little like a rattler, too. Our cotton mouths though, will go defensive if you're anywhere near their nest. How did you discover this place?"

"My first visit was with a friend from grade school. His family used to come on weekends and I tagged along. Later, after I could drive, I'd just come here to get away by myself."

"Ever bring a girl here?" I ask matter-of-factly.

"Why, are you curious?" he replies with his own question.

"Was that a yes?" I ask with a smile.

"Yes. I once brought my wife, Lydia, during our first and only year of marriage. She's not an outdoorsy person, so it wasn't exactly her idea of a good time. Now you know why she lives in London. You ready to swim back?" We jump back in and swim across at a leisurely pace.

"I'm famished and whipped," I declare to him as I stagger back to the blanket. "This is more exercise than I've had in months." I wrap up in my beach towel and sit down on the blanket to spread out the food containers from the backpack.

"I see Jamie prepared us a feast. Oh good; he's sent some of his garden chutney for our sandwiches; you ready for one?"

After we eat, we pick up our trash and change clothes. It's so beautiful here that I want to linger a while and return to the blanket. The day is young and I have yet to bring Thom into conversation about our relationship and the wedding; there'll never be a better time than right now.

"Thom...," I begin but he tries to open a conversation at the same time.

"Sarah...I'm sorry...no, go ahead." He laughs and remains still.

"I can wait, please, you go ahead."

"Very well, I want to bring you up to date on the Mill and some other things..." He stumbles a little on the last part.

"What other things?"

"First of all, it appears we've found a way through the design error and the contractor begins next week with an addendum to the original plans. We're adding a large panel of dormers to the waterside roof which should solve our problem."

"That's wonderful news Thom, you must be feeling relieved." I give him a hug.

"Yes, on that subject I am. But to every upside in life, there's a downside. There's no easy way to tell you this, so here goes. The Estate Trust is in nasty shape and so are Dad's personal resources. Because of all the above, I decided to use some of my personal savings to finish and open the Mill."

"But Thom, it's wonderful you're able to do that; why are you so down about it?"

"Because, it will limit you and me financially after we're married and I may not be able to support you in the style of life I've been used to, for a few years at least." He leans back against a tree in silence.

"I see two problems here Thom; one, that you think I'd be put off by news that I can't live in a manor house and send our children to the best schools, which actually would be my life normally. And two...," he interrupts me.

"Sarah, that's not what I meant. I love you and I want to give you everything that I've enjoyed in life."

"I know that about you Thom and I love you all the more for wanting to do it." I rethink how to express myself without hurting his feelings.

"Thom, I've worked hard over the past few months to get established on my own and feel solid in my own right. I want to be accepted as your equal partner in our marriage; if you can't handle that, then maybe we aren't as well suited to each other as I thought."

He reaches out and wraps his arms around me.

"You're not going to leave me, are you?" he asks.

"No, I'm not, Thom; I look forward to a long life with you, but please come into the twenty-first century with your views on a woman's role in the home." I draw back to look at him.

"Apparently, you don't realize I'm the kind of woman who wants to be included in decisions that affect us both; like the Estate, our personal finances, our home, and our children.

"We're not married yet, so this latest decision of yours doesn't 'count', but for the record, I think you did the right thing," I tell him truthfully.

"You do?" he asks.

"Yes, and since we're on the subject, I may as well tell you there's something else."

He drops his arms, "What 'else'; how many things are you dissatisfied about in me?" he asks, his face flushed.

"That, right there, is the last," I reply. "If you believe I love you then discussing and resolving problems between us should be easier to talk through without rankling anyone's defenses."

He looks at me without speaking for a few seconds then says, "There may be another problem."

"What do you mean? "I ask.

"Our honeymoon plans may suffer a downsizing." He goes glum again.

"Will you stop with the ups and downs?" I beg him. "We'll work our way through this and besides, you have nothing to worry about from me by downsizing; this is more about you, isn't it?"

"Yes, it may be...I thought we were well on the way to joining our lives. Now I'm getting the distinct impression you're having second thoughts; are you Sarah?"

"No, I'm not, Thom and please don't project your doubts on me; if you're having second thoughts," I say softly, " then we need to talk about them." I try to touch his face, but he sits back to look at me then stands up.

"For the 'record' as you put it," he says, "you're the only one, other than Dad, who's ever been able to talk straight with me and I value your opinions, I really do. I'm just coming to realise that people can't stand alone forever.

"Dad's sudden news about Highbridge and the changes we must make are tough to handle. It's the only life-style I've ever known and the event has thrown me...I've been an island for a long time and any change is difficult." He pauses to look at me then extends his hands to help me up from the blanket.

"This much is clear to me Sarah; as long as you're beside me I can work through all of it, come whatever life style we're destined for. I'm sorry I come off looking like a pompous ass sometimes; can you forgive me? I'll work on my attitude beginning today; can you be patient a little longer and give me another chance?"

"I can, Mr. Smith," I tell him, "if you promise never again to think I don't love you enough to be by your side."

"I promise you that my dear," he says with a smile and seals it with a kiss.

Back at my cottage after dinner with Thomas and his family, I change to pajamas to watch television in bed and relax before sleep.

My cat jumps up to join me and collects some petting while he has me figuratively cornered. Poor tiger has all but been replaced by work and my fiancé. He turns over for a tummy rub then goes to the foot of the bed for his evening nap before night prowling later and I return to the telly.

Thomas and our exchange of words earlier keep coming to mind. It certainly wasn't what I'd planned; *our first real 'discussion'* I think as I deny it was an argument; but it could have turned into one if he hadn't sincerely apologized and confirmed his love for me.

And isn't that what's needed in a relationship? I ask myself; two people willing to meet half-way and see problems objectively? It dawns on me that we did that today.

So what's stopping you Sandlin? I ask myself and the answer comes back loud and clear...*Nothing.*

I enter the now-familiar number to Thom's cell phone and wait. It's late, about eleven but I'm sure he's still up.

"Hello..." I hear a muffled voice say and confirm that no, he's sleeping.

"Oh, I'm so sorry, you were sleeping weren't you? Just go back to sleep, I'll call you in the morning."

"What...wait...Sarah, is that you? Just a minute." I hear him say then nothing else until the phone hits something.

"Sarah, are you still there? Sorry, I dropped you on the floor, I mean; the phone fell off the edge."

"I didn't think you'd be in bed yet," I tell him.

"No, I fell asleep on the couch here in the great room. No problem; are you alright?" he asks.

"Yes, of course. I just wanted to talk, that's all."

"Well, here I am; what's up?"

"Something occurred to me about our exchange this morning," I say.

"Oh, you mean our argument; what about it?" he asks.

"I think we handled a difficult subject very well and resolved the issues; what do you think?"

"I feel good about it."

"Good, me-too, although I've already said as much..." I cringe at the absurdity. "Anyway, it's opened a door for me, Thom."

"What do you mean?" he asks.

"I mean, in a way, I've been holding back, letting old experiences influence how I've related to you over the past few months."

"I've felt that but couldn't isolate a reason and thought it was me," he admits. "Care to tell me more?"

"Yes, I think I owe you that, my dear." I proceed to tell him more about how I lived the eleven years after Brian's death, up to the time Thomas' letter arrived.

"Sarah, I had no idea how closed up your life was, or how important my letter would be. You know I sent it spur-of-the-moment and questioned my sanity for weeks afterward until you called me," he admits.

"You never told me that, but I can understand your doubts since it had been a long time since we'd seen each other. When I visited Brian at school, you only sort of met me in passing while vacating the apartment you two shared."

"So are we good now my Sarah; no more confessions to be made?" he asks.

"Yes, I can say without hesitation we're good, Thom."

"Then I'm asking the question again in a slightly less than adequate, romantic setting; Sarah Sandlin, I love you, will you marry me...soon?"

"I would love to; let's talk dates." I tell him with an unseen smile over the phone.

"How about in the fall before the cold weather sets in?" He suggests.

"Perfect; I love you, too, Thom. Goodnight my dear."

We disconnect for the night but my heart is beating so quickly I can't get to sleep.

There's the dress, flowers, reception, a honeymoon spot; all seem to pull on me at once.

At last I sit straight up in bed with an idea.

My cat Tom looks up from his nest at the foot of the bed in askance; *what are you up to?*

"I'm going to buy a bridal magazine...maybe two...or three." I tell him but he contains his excitement and returns to sleep with no reaction.

"You're right; I'll wait until morning." I lay back down, a changed woman forever.

Chapter Six – Alliances

"Pat, darling?" Gloria calls from her chair in the lanai.

"Yes, dear" I answer.

"Could you come here for a moment?"

I close up my murder mystery and put it aside. Forty-two years with this woman and I still scramble to her side when she beckons. She hasn't lost her appeal and I know she thinks the same of me. Our retirement to this island condo has been all we expected and more.

"What is it?" I drop a kiss on the top of her head.

"This article in the Island News; it's a historical piece on an art gallery established here in the late 1800's. Look at the name of the couple – Briana and Patrick Gordon. Honey, I believe Gordon is the name Sarah mentioned in her research for the Smiths."

"You're kidding! We better send this to her."

"Send, yes, but call her now;" My lovely wife orders me, "this may be something she can use right away."

I enter the now-familiar number for Sarah in the U.K. Since she moved last December and we met the Smith's at Christmas, we've had a special place in our hearts for the entire family. Our holiday at Highbridge was phenomenal and we look forward to going again this year.

"Hello Sarah, it's your Dad. How are you sweetheart?" I ask her.

"Hi Dad; great to hear your voice, is everything okay?" she asks.

"Yes of course. I was instructed to phone by you-know-who, but it's good to hear you too, sweetheart; all good there?" I ask her.

"Yes it is; as a matter of fact, we're talking wedding dates today."

"That's wonderful Sarah, but I need to hand you over to your mother now before she hits me with a newspaper; just kidding, she's boring a hole in me with her eyes."

"Here you go," I say and hand the phone to Gloria.

"Hi Dear, it's Mom."

"Hi Mom, I'd know your voice anywhere."

"I had Dad call you for a reason, but you go first and tell me what the 'wonderful' news is that you two talked about."

"Thomas and I are working on a date for the wedding," Sarah tells me with laughter in her voice.

"Oh, that is good news; when are you thinking at this point?" I ask.

"Maybe in the early fall, before the nasty weather arrives," she answers.

"Good idea, although we enjoyed Christmas so much last year; whatever you decide though dear, just give us time to reserve flights."

"I will Mom. Now are you going to tell me what you called about?" she gently reminds me.

"Yes; oh my goodness, I almost forgot with your news. Today's paper has an article on an art shop here during the late 1800's. It was established by a Briana and Patrick Gordon. It says they came from Aberdeen; didn't you mention a Gordon family in Thomas's history?"

"Yes," Sarah answers, "we believe his fifth-removed grandfather may have remarried a Gordon. It's just hard to believe it could be this easy though, Mom. But send me the article, actually, the whole newspaper. I'd like the editor's name and the name of the person who wrote the article, so just send the whole thing," Sarah says in one breath.

She's excited I think with a smile. "Okay, we'll get it in the mail tomorrow, special delivery so it'll get there quickly."

"Thanks Mom, I appreciate that. Isn't it funny how you find things in the last place you expect to look; sort of how Thom and I met. Mom, I'm so happy with him."

"I can tell dear and we're happy for you. Is there something we can do to help with the wedding?"

"Can't think of anything right now, but I'll keep you in mind. You guys take care, I love you."

"We love you too dear; bye now." I hang up with tears in my eyes.

"What's wrong Gloria?" Pat asks me.

"Nothing; our daughter is happy...it's just so wonderful. Come here you and give me a hug; I'll be fine."

I savor the warmth of my husband's arms and the good feeling that everything is finally right for our daughter now. She suffered grief for so long after her husband's death; thank God, Thomas came into her life when he did.

"Good morning Miss Sarah." Berty meets me inside the front door at Highbridge and takes my umbrella for deposit to the large chinoiserie jar in the corner.

"Good morning Berty; is Thomas around?"

"I believe he's in the kitchen, Miss."

On my way to the back stairs, I pause at the great room to say hello to Meg who sits at her desk working on her computer. I admire the flood of sunlight shining through the French doors down the length of the large room; it's joined with the light from the second floor windows and fully illuminates the room's furnishings.

Two fireplaces hold forth at either end, their stone faces carved with hunt scenes from a bygone era. Several large paintings depict the surrounding countryside as it must have been when the Estate was built including one of the Copper Swift flowing through forested land before it was cleared for farming.

The upholsteries of the various couches and chairs reflect the rich colors of the oriental carpet beneath them and I recall how perfect last Christmas's celebration was in here. I can't wait to see a giant tree decorated again and the wide eyes of the children from the village.

"You're an early bird," Meg says as she comes from behind her desk to greet me.

"Don't let me interrupt you," I beg of her, "I'm just here looking for Thom."

"Don't be silly, I need a break and besides, there's coffee in the kitchen." She smiles and takes my arm to walk the hallway.

Thomas, Joe and Stephen sit at the table when Meg and I arrive; they're obviously enjoying something as if it's been months since their last meal.

"Boys; good morning," I say. The three mutter something unintelligible with their mouths full, but Thomas swallows quickly, wipes his mouth and gives me a good morning kiss.

"You've got to taste these Sarah, they are so good." He pulls out chairs for Meg and me.

"If Jamie made them, I believe you; hey Jamie," I greet him as he brings more coffee to the table for us.

"Good morning Miss Sarah, Mrs. Smith, what can I get for you? Please help yourselves to the cross buns, there's plenty, although there were more about ten minutes ago." He smiles as Stephen and Joe look up innocently.

"Et Tu Brutus?" Thomas directs to Jamie, who laughs.

Then he turns to me; "We've only had one apiece, maybe two," He confesses, "I promise you Sarah."

"If you want to continue fibbing like that with any credibility," I tease him, "you'll need to get a signed confidentiality statement from Jamie, but on to the reason I'm here. Guess what my parents found in their local newspaper?" I can't wait on his guessing game and continue.

"Look at this article and tell me who it might be." Thom recognises the name at once.

"Gordon–isn't that the name you saw on a marriage certificate from Aberdeen?" he asks.

"Yes, on the marriage records of a Daniel Smith and Philomena Gordon, so the Patrick in this article could be related to her. I can't confirm it yet, but it's worth a look. The Gordon clan was strong in the Aberdeen area which won't make it easy, but there's good genealogy already on record which will help. Remember, Emily said Charles had a great aunt who lived in St. Thomas and this could be her," I remind him.

"Fascinating" Stephen speaks as he leaves the table, "Sarah, please pass along my thanks to Pat and Gloria when you speak with them, won't you?"

"Yes, of course."

"Are we ready to tour the Mill?" he asks Thom and Joe then adds, "You ladies have a good nosh; we'll see you later."

After they leave, I give in to temptation and take one of the cross buns that created such a stir. One bite and I understand what the 'boys' were up against; these are still warm and positively addictive. The pastry dough is soft and buttery, laced with cinnamon, brown sugar, currants and on its top a generous dollop of white icing. I eat slowly and sip coffee while Meg and I talk between bites.

"Has Stephen talked about the Estate and its finances to you lately?" I ask her, deliberately casual, in case he hasn't. "Thom told me last week he's finishing the Mill with his own funds; nothing in detail, though," I add.

"Stephen came to me after they worked it all out," she answers. "He's realised he needs to trust his son and heir's judgement and has allowed Thomas equal access to the books and investments for the Estate."

"Ah. I told Thomas last evening not to worry about me; I was raised in middle-class America. But I did call attention to the fact that he should adopt a more conservative life-style and he admits he's having trouble with that."

"I know what you mean Sarah; Stephen still holds the values he was raised with and feels responsible for the well-being of everyone in the household and to some extent, those in the surrounding farms and village." She sips her coffee, "You're very wise to understand the problems Thom faces."

"It became clear as we talked that Thom shares Stephen's values," I tell her. "I admire them both for that, I really do. But they have to realise that unless they cut back on expenses here, there's a real threat to their maintaining ownership in the future. Tough words, but from what I've seen so far, there are too many deserted mansions and estates already out there whose owners couldn't save them."

"What was his response, if I may ask?" Meg inquires.

"He acknowledged he has a problem dealing with the reduction in funds and asked that I bring it to his attention when I notice him 'going overboard', so to speak."

"And your reply my dear?" Meg asks.

"I told him I'm willing, as long as he takes my advice seriously. I'm not naïve enough to think I can change him but he'll need support in his efforts to adjust and I'll do whatever I can to help. I'd like to be considered an equal partner and he already knows I expect an equal say in our personal financial decisions after we're married.

"And on that subject Meg, we're setting a date for the wedding! My parents already know as of last night, but I haven't had the opportunity to tell you and Stephen."

"That's wonderful dear, I'm happy for you both." She looks at me and reaches across the table to pat my hand.

"I believe you're the best thing to happen to Thomas and to this family in a very long time and I have no doubt you'll be a huge asset to him and to our family."

"Thank-you Megs; I think the world of you and Stephen, too."

She hesitates, "It may not be easy as a modern woman in this household where so many have gone before and played the subservient wife, but we're both up to the task, don't you agree?"

"I do Meg and certainly two modern women are better than one, do you also agree?" I giggle a little at the idea of our pairing up to make our goals clearer to the men.

"Oh, I certainly do Sarah," she confirms and we laugh together at our pact.

"How do you feel about this big old home?" Meg asks me.

"The Estate is...like living a fairy tale. I love it and appreciate it. I don't even mind the lack of central heat; the fireplaces and the occasional space heater do fine for me. What do you think of it, Meg?"

"I've loved it from the first time I came to help Irene with the employee parties. I never imagined living here, coming from meager beginnings in London. As a child, I always had enough to eat and a roof over my head but mum and da worked hard for everything we had; I suppose it was comparable to the working class level in America at that time.

"When Stephen brought me here last year, "she continues, "it felt like I'd retired to some luxurious hotel. These last few months, I've finally let myself think of this as home; of course, marrying Stephen has a lot to do with that." She smiles that lovely smile of hers.

"Have you thought about what he and Thomas will do if the manor can't be saved?" I ask her.

"No, and Stephen has never gone there; it would be extremely hard for them both."

"Yes, I agree. Personally, I'll do all I can to help avoid that and I have some ideas to offset costs around here. As the women of the house, we should put our ideas together to come up with a plan, just in case it comes down to it. Are you with me Meg?"

"You bet," she answers, "as long as we promise not to discuss our plans with our husbands individually. We should bring our ideas to them in a joint meeting so they don't think we're conspiring against their roles at the Estate."

"We're both smarter than that Meg, but yes, I agree whole-heartedly." I cross my heart and raise my hand; Meg does the same.

Then she smiles, "Now, about the wedding, Sarah; what have you already done and what do you need from me?"

Later, I walk to my desk in the corner of the Library by the family record shelves. Thomas provided this desk on my first visit last year and though I have a small working study in the guest room of my cottage, I still enjoy coming here to continue research on his family.

"Sarah." Stephen enters the doorway in his brusque style. "I thought you might be here."

"What can I do for you, Stephen?"

"These letters of my father's you found last year in the attic; I'd completely forgotten to return them to you as promised."

"That's alright Stephen, I knew you would eventually; plenty of other work to keep me busy here, but thank-you, I'll enjoy reading them.

"I've wanted to ask you something," I continue, "do you have a minute?"

"What is it my dear?"

"Now that I'm to be one of the Mrs. Smiths in your family, accepting pay for 'our' family research would be uncomfortable for me. I have paying accounts now and will be picking up more; after I'm officially clear of my Visa, we'll dispense with your generous retainer."

He looks surprised but before he can reply, I quickly add, "The research will be personal at that point Stephen and I'll continue in it for many years." I don't let him know I've begun to see ways to lower expenses for the Estate and consider this as one item ticked off my list.

"That wasn't 'officially' a question was it Sarah." He smiles at me before going on, "You really are a gift you know, in Thomas's life and in mine. You see I get to watch my son be happy and for a father that is paramount; thank-you, Sarah."

"My thanks to you as well Stephen, you made all this possible and I can't think of anyplace I'd rather be than here with Thomas and your family."

Chapter Seven – Tiptoeing Again

The contents of the tin box have proven interesting as apparently my 'friend' in the closet knew they would be. I refer to my ghostly accomplice as a friend because he hasn't proven otherwise...yet. I pause at the thought.

The tin box contained letters from a Regis Smith to an Angus Smith who might be a previous owner, if not the original owner and builder of Highbridge. Regis' address to Angus in the letters leaves no doubt in my mind that he is Angus' son.

Regis was with the British Army in India when he wrote the letters, their dates fall between June 1934 and September 1935. I'm enough of a history buff to know there were frequent clashes between the British Army stationed in northern India and the tribes of that time.

One of the letters in particular is quite touching and to my interest.

Dear Father,

It's been a long and exhausting day and we are at last encamped after six miles over rough terrain. Some officers who were initially trained here refer to this region as the 'grim' and the name certainly fits. We've marched east to join with two other columns in the Khaisora Valley as a show of force. Unfortunately, Pathan tribes opened fire on us in the river valley and we fought hard to reach the village of Bichhe Kashkal. We've been told one of the other columns, has encountered similar if not heavier action and is delayed at least a day in joining us; we've lost over a hundred men plus our pack mules which makes supplies short.

So I must write this, though I know it will cause you pain. If I do not return, I want you to know you've always been the best father I could ever have asked for. Despite the fact that I failed to be the one to follow in your footsteps at the Company, you never discouraged me in my military career and for that I am grateful. You are a fair and generous man and have nothing to be sad about in my bringing up or training. I have a stubbornness born of my own determination and if I die, a military man through, as all who fight here, I realise it is my duty and my mission to lay down my life if need be.

Should this be my last letter to you, I pray you will continue to watch over Charles though he has given us every reason to believe he is a fine and honorable man and follows in your footsteps to my satisfaction. There is not another man I would rather he emulate, than you.

I am assured you will pass the shell to Charles in my stead and explain what must be done in future to preserve and protect it.

You have my unfailing love – in hope that we shall see each other soon.

Your faithful son - Regis

That last bit holds my attention. I wonder...what did he mean by 'assured you will pass the shell to Charles in my stead'?

I stop to breathe in the fresh cool air while thoughts of Sarah and our picnic last week run through my mind. There's a spring in my step this morning as I walk down to the Mill. It rained last night and the road's dust has turned to mud; it clings to my wellies but I really don't care.

She's so beautiful I think and has nothing to be shy of in a swimsuit either. It would be difficult to put her image out of my mind but why would I? She's consented to be my wife and it's natural to look forward to sharing each other's love. She surely senses that at her signal, I would bring her to me as a lover, but she brought us both back to reality, as it should be since we've agreed to wait until after we're married.

I continue down the road to the Mill but again think how much I admire the way she's perfectly at ease in a crowd of strangers or with family at Highbridge. Her natural, unaffected manner and the laughter we share is a joy.

Below, the Mill lies easy on the edge of Copper Swift; its windows reflect the sun coming over the hill behind me. Beyond the Swift, wire fences shine and weave around the green fields of neighboring farms; smoke rises from their chimneys as Aga's are ramped up and daily chores begin.

She's no shy violet either I think; bold enough to tell me her expectations for our marriage and to help me see more objectively as I adjust to the Estate's changes. God, how I admire her for that and what promise she holds as an advisor, strong supporter and someday, a mother for our children. *She really is everything I could ever want or need* I conclude.

Birds fly noisy overhead on their way to field and river and prompt me to move along. I become aware that all is right in the world today, at least here in my part of it.

Joe's already with the contractor on the second floor and I smile when I see the amended blueprints spread out before them on a makeshift table.

"Morning, looks like you're heavy into it, don't let me interrupt," I tell them.

"No problem Thomas, we were just reviewing the updated plans," Joes says.

"Good idea – morning Bill."

"Mr. Smith." He comes to shake my hand, "We can finish the project in another week, barring any holdups."

"Spare me the "h" word, please." I beg with a hearty laugh, "We'll have no more of those."

"Meg, what's your schedule look like today?"

"Well actually, I'm pretty well caught up; what's on your mind Sarah?" She asks from her desk.

"How would you like to help me shop for a wedding gown?"

"I'd love to," she replies with glee, "I'm so honored you'd ask."

"I'm honored you'd consent to be dragged through every store in York. If we don't find one there, we're on our way to Manchester, but we can pace ourselves and do that another day."

"I know a perfectly lovely shop in York and feel sure you'll find something; but if you don't, she also does custom dresses," Meg replies.

"Wonderful; I forgot you probably know every seamstress between here and London, since you were in the business with your husband."

"Well, that was many years ago, but I did occasionally shop for formal wear when Stephen and his wife hosted their holiday parties."

"Ah, Thomas's descriptions of their 'do's' made them sound quite lovely," I recall.

"They always knew how to make everyone feel welcome; just the right amount of decorum, but not stuffy; you know what I mean? Anyway, what time shall we leave?" She checks her watch. "We really should get going; it's already ten o'clock."

"Good; I'll get my purse from the library and we'll be off." I'm so excited at the prospect of finding 'the' dress, I can hardly wait.

We make the drive to York in good time and Meg parks in a lot, a short walk from the bridal shop.

"This city is charming," I say as I exit the car, "wonderful historical preservation."

"Yes, I suppose." Meg laughs.

"You don't sound so sure about that," I chide and wait for her on the sidewalk.

"It's just that you're seeing it through new eyes Sarah. You know how it is; if you're raised in the area and lived there most of your life, it's a little less impressive. But yes, it does have quite the history. Like many places in the U.K., the Romans were here as you can see by the walls and gates."

"I see there are two universities; that must help raise revenue for the city."

"It does; when classes are in session the population goes up by about forty-thousand plus."

"I underestimated the schools' sizes," I tell her.

"Did you see the York Minster Cathedral as we came in? It's the largest medieval gothic cathedral in northern Europe. If you love stained glass, you should take a tour someday; you'll be suitably impressed, believe me," Meg says.

I'm in love with the stone streets and sidewalks as we continue through a streetscape so full of charm I can barely pass a shop without stopping. There are small lace shops, tea rooms and sweet shops, in every niche of the narrow street and Meg has her hands full keeping me on track.

At last we arrive at the bridal shop tucked into the first and second floors of a vintage storefront right out of a Dickens novel. The front bay window is multi-paned and displays a beautiful gown of satin and lace we stop to admire before entering.

"Good day." An attendant greets us cheerfully and then recognizes Meg.

"Margaret; how wonderful to see you," she declares with a wide smile and they embrace. "How long has it been? Fifteen years?"

"Oh, at least, but let's not count, shall we? How have you been Peg? Forgive me, this is a friend of mine, Sarah Sandlin; Sarah, Peggy Marquart, the proprietress."

"Any friend of Meg's is certainly welcome," she declares and kisses both my cheeks in the European manner, my first such greeting.

"Come sit down; may I bring you some tea?" she asks.

"That would be lovely Peg," Meg answers, "I'll show Sarah around while we wait."

"You know the place as well as I do Megs; I won't be a moment."

The dress in the window has a rather lengthy train which wasn't obvious from our view outside.

"Beautiful isn't it?" Meg says as she joins me.

"Yes, it is, especially if you're going all out on a grand scale, but under the circumstances, a little less grand is in order, at least a dress that fits through a normal door or into a vehicle."

"To be sure, but you haven't really told me what you have in mind Sarah."

"And that's what I'd like to hear as well." Peg returns with the tea service and places the tray in front of an upholstered bank of seating.

"Let's get caught up, shall we?" she invites. "Big wedding...small intimate wedding...something in-between?"

"In-between for our village Church," I reply. "It's where Thomas was baptized and the family has historically attends services there."

"Very nice; have you determined a date?" Peggy asks.

"We've decided to reserve during the Christmas season." I look at Meg and see her smile.

"That should give us enough time for the Church and accommodate all that needs doing," Meg adds.

"It should, but let's not get too comfortable; that's still a rather tight schedule," Peggy warns, "especially with the holidays. Better not delay in reserving the Church; you won't be the only one with the same idea and things have a way of taking on a life of their own at this stage."

"You're right, and I will push ahead with the help of my friends and parents; though Mom is far away, she'll be thoroughly involved," I laugh.

"There'll be a required visit with the Vicar since you're not a national and a special license will have to be applied for," Peggy adds. "But the Vicar will tell you all about that."

I didn't know my being here with a Visa wouldn't be enough and file the information away for my to-do list.

"Let's go upstairs and get started, shall we? We'll try some different styles to see what you really want and go from there." Peggy leads us up a small stair to the second floor where many ready-made gowns line the walls. High windows let light pour in from the north, almost like an artist's loft; the various shades and colors in the dresses are beautiful.

"I'm intrigued by the blush colors, maybe a pale blue? If not, then an off-white, but not in the beige family," I add.

"I have two in blush and I'll put them in the dressing room for you now," Peg tells me. "Go ahead and look through the dresses to see if any others interest you; look for style as well as color. If you find a style you like, we can perhaps order in a different color."

"Thank-you, Peggy." The large numbers of choices around me are overwhelming.

"Okay," I declare to Meg, "I'm going in."

She laughs, "If you'd like, I can start over here on this side and hold up any that strike me as potentials?"

"Good idea."

I've spent the last two hours in the dressing room. One dress, a misty blue, is really the color I want but the style isn't me; too elaborate, too much train and it makes me look fat. Peggy checked but it isn't available in any other style. I take it off to try another, a 'mermaid' style – really not me.

Spent from the rigors of the 'try-on', I at last face the fact that it will not be today I find my dress and break the news to Meg.

"We need another day," I tell her. "I'm sorry but I can't reach a decision on any of these."

"Now don't worry Sarah, we can certainly visit some different shops; Peg is a seasoned veteran at this and understands. You're no different from any other bride and want the dress that truly feels special."

"Thanks Meg, I'll get dressed and we'll reserve a new day to try again." Disappointed, tired, but not beaten I vow to continue my hunt through the month ahead until I find 'the one'.

"Darling, you look absolutely worn out," Thomas remarks as I enter the kitchen. Great I think as I realise it's been four weeks of unsuccessful shopping since Meg and I started...and still no dress.

"Thanks for the compliment," I growl as I attempt a jest, but fail miserably.

"We've searched again, but haven't had any luck." Meg fills in the blanks on my behalf.

"I'm sorry," he takes me in his arms, "Don't worry, you'll find the right one. If we need to, we can motor down to London to one of the larger salons."

"Thomas, do you remember our conversation at the lake last month?" I whisper into his ear.

"Oh...well, um...that is," he blunders around for the right words until I rescue him before the others in the room hear.

"It's alright Thom; there are other shops in the area." I appear cheerful despite my wearied state, "I just need more time."

"Of course, you're right." He kisses me on the forehead like a child. "I've heard every woman has experienced the dress hunt, even my mother had to have a gown custom-made to her preferences. I know you'll find one Sarah."

He has more confidence than I do.

Later, I notice the letters on my desk that Stephen returned to me weeks ago; I haven't given them a look-over yet, with all my dress hunting and decide to do so before returning to the cottage this evening

I casually shuffle through the ten-odd envelopes to view their dates and notice that on four of them, not only does the handwriting change but their dates are of an earlier era. I sit up straighter and turn on the desk lamp.

These are from nineteen thirty-five and thirty-six I notice with surprise; how did Stephen miss them? And then it dawns on me; he didn't read any of them, that's how. At first I'm surprised and a little disappointed in him, but as I reconsider, it isn't such a big thing. After all, the man retired last year, has totally redone his life, married, planned the Mill with Thomas and lately addressed the finances of the Estate. He's certainly well-covered with valid excuses for inattention to vintage mail. I forgive him and move my attention back to the letters.

These are from a Regis Smith to our Angus Smith. *He's Angus's son* I declare after reading his remarks to his father. He's in the British Army in India—one of the medals found in the trunk last year. Too excited to sit still and focus, I put the letter carefully back into its envelope to share with Thomas.

I'm up the stairs in under a minute and knock at his door. He opens it wrapped in a towel and immediately checks to make sure the towel is anchored.

"Sarah, I'm just out of the shower, can you wait a few minutes?"

"Yes, of course, I just have something to show you, go do what you need to," I direct and come in to wait at the fireside.

"You haven't decided some earth-shattering change on the wedding date have you, because I'm ready to go whenever you are?" He calls from the depths of the marble-lined bathroom. I'm glad someone is, I think wryly then answer him.

"No, nothing like that; we're still on track for December."

"Well then, what is it that brings you to my door madam?" he asks from just behind me and causes me to jump.

"Thomas, stop sneaking up on me like that." But he already has me in a warm cozy hug against his terry robe.

"Explain yourself," he jokes then turns me around to kiss me within an inch of my life.

"I forget," I say as I return for more. Time continues until I realise what I said.

"That is, I have something really surprising and out of the blue to show you." I hold up the letters to him.

He smiles and releases me, "Something out of the blue, now that I want to see." He dries his hair with a towel while I take the letters over to his desk and turn on the lamp. He follows me to read a few.

"These are amazing, Sarah."

"Aren't they?" I confirm. "Here's the thing, your Dad didn't say a word about all these older letters; I don't think he read any of them and just returned them to me as promised."

"He's been rather busy this past year," Thom says as he hangs the damp towel over the end of the bed.

"I realise that and have already forgiven him. What are the chances that the very documents that provide proof of his great grandfather were in his hands and he didn't know it?" I begin to calm down now that the secret is out.

"And here's the other thing," I add. "How did these letters join those we found in the library last year? I examined the envelopes thoroughly after we pulled them out and there were none with these dates and change of handwriting."

"You're saying these were not with the others in the secret shelf space?" he asks in surprise.

"That's exactly what I'm saying. Someone added these to the bundle after I gave them to Stephen."

"But why would anyone do that? Do you think it was Dad?"

"He'd be the most logical since the letters have been in his possession for almost nine months."

"But there's a flaw in that theory and you said it yourself; he was too busy to read them and returned them to you. I can't imagine his being deceptive about it and to what end? I don't think he knew of these." He stops to think about it then adds, "If you didn't see them right out of the secret shelf in the library, then someone put them in later."

"A little late on the draw there sir, but I agree." He starts to playfully grab me but I elude him and open the door. "Love you – see you later. I'm off to the cottage."

"Sure you don't want to stay a while?" He wears his best puppy-dog look for my benefit.

"Not sure, but nevertheless good night Thom." I say as I leave him, "See you tomorrow."

I've read through all the letters this morning over coffee at my kitchen table, except the last two; such touching correspondence between Angus and his son Regis. It's clear that Angus watched over and practically raised Charles during Regis' absence in the military.

It's exciting to find an added generation and confirms what I've suspicioned all along; there had to be an additional male in the line somewhere to make the dates work and my earlier timeline can now be updated with Charles' true father, Regis. One thing certain, I need to study the British Army in India and learn more about the places he described. It'll add depth to the period for me and help with finding more documentation on both Regis and Charles.

I have to stop now and put the letters away; Thomas and I are scheduled to meet the Vicar this afternoon to reserve our wedding date. One nice thing I've learned is that the Church of England recognizes other faiths and will wed us; there are no required religious classes to 'bring me into the fold' from my Baptist upbringing, unless of course I'm interested. I haven't dismissed the idea and want to adopt a church soon; why not my new family's church? I remember what Peggy said about the special license requirement and hope it won't be a problem, but we'll find out today.

Chapter Eight - The Road to Marriage

Thomas and I arrive at the vicarage at half past three. We're a little early so we walk to the nearby Church to admire its beautiful exterior architecture and stained glass windows. It's smaller than St Machar's in Aberdeen where we visited last year. What a beautiful place that was, but this lovely church will be perfect for us and we return to the vicarage just in time for our appointment.

"Good afternoon Thomas." The Vicar opens the door and welcomes us both warmly. "It's been a while my boy," he remarks.

Thomas reminds me of a little boy caught in error as he looks self-consciously at his shoes before he answers.

"What can I say, Sir; yes it has, no excuses."

"Well, thank-you for sparing me those," the Vicar says easily. "You're welcome here at any time, you know that after all these years. And who do we have here?" He faces me and I hold out my hand to him.

"This is my fiancée, Sarah Sandlin."

"How do you do Sir," I greet him.

"Well, well; do I detect an American accent?" He asks as he shakes my hand.

"Yes sir, I'm here on Visa as an employee of Stephen's for research into his family's history."

"You're the one working with two other families in our congregation I believe?" He remarks.

"Yes, I am."

"Wonderful. Won't you both come with me and we'll sit down for a chat." He leads us to a small office off the sitting room with a lovely soft light from two windows. The room is simply furnished; a medium-sized, mahogany desk, two padded chairs and several file cabinets along one wall nearly fill the space. Various pictures of past officials in the Church as well as photos of events and congregation fill another wall.

"This is just beautiful," I remark.

"Yes, I'm very blessed to have a workspace here," the Vicar tells me, "I enjoy it every day; puts me in the mood for my work, you might say.

"Now I like to get acquainted with the couples I marry; just a little basic information to see where you've come from and your expectations for marriage. It allows me to work on foreseeable legal requirements as well. Don't panic; I do this with every couple and so far no one has 'failed' my scrutiny. I'm sure everything will be fine but better to go in 'eyes wide open' eh?" he asks.

Thom and I answer with "Of course" and the Vicar proceeds.

"Thomas, I know you've been married before and if I'm not mistaken, that was annulled, was it not?"

"Yes, you actually helped with that and have the records here I believe," he answers quickly.

"Ah yes, I remember Lydia, very nice girl. Whatever happened to her?"

"She works in London; we keep in touch during the holidays, still friends," Thom answers. "It's been over ten years since we made the decision and it was the right thing to do."

"No regrets?" the Vicar asks.

"No regrets, sir, for either of us."

"I've known you and your father for a very long time and believe I can count on you to tell me the truth; therefore Thomas I have no qualms in accepting what you say." He then turns to me.

"Sarah, tell me a little about yourself; I understand you're from Florida originally?" He surprises me with the question.

"Yes, I am but how did you know?"

"My dear, when you live in a small town and are engaged to a member of their only venerable family, word tends to get around." He smiles then asks, "Have you been married previously?"

"Yes I have. I lost Brian to cancer eleven years ago."

"I'm very sorry for your loss my dear. And was it a happy marriage?"

"It was; we were young and very much in love with plans for family and the future but that was all taken away in a few months."

He takes my hand and holds it, "How did you handle that grief Sarah?"

I'm surprised he would ask but trust he has good reason to bring it up.

"I didn't handle it at all for several years. I stayed at home, only saw my parents periodically, mostly let the grief own me. A friend of mine came to my rescue one evening and allowed me to rant uninterrupted for the first time since his death. By doing so she helped me to finally get beyond it, at least to see daylight and accept a job she offered me."

"A good friend indeed; and how are you now, Sarah?" the Vicar asks.

"Last October, I visited Thomas and his family then returned home to the States because I thought I belonged there. But it was only a week before I realised I loved him and I'd been truly happy with him here. When I admitted it to myself, it was as though Brian were telling me 'it's okay to leave'. I sold my house, bought another here in the Village and returned to make a new life; I haven't regretted it."

"Well Thomas, looks like you have a determined woman here," he laughs then adds, "and very sincere in her love for you my son."

"I know that sir," Thomas replies as he looks at me. "I feel the same about her."

"Good. Now that we have that cleared up, let's move on to joining you two together, shall we? Sarah, what religious faith do you claim?

"I was raised Methodist then went to Baptist. Currently, I'm sort of between churches." I feel guilty telling the Vicar but want to be truthful.

"I see; thank-you for being honest Sarah. I hope when you pick up the trail again, you'll keep us in mind? We're always available for consult, so-to-speak and welcome all members of all religions to services."

He doesn't wait for an answer but immediately starts to rummage in his desk.

"Now what did I do with that information pack...oh yes, here it is." He pulls a paper notebook from one of his desk drawers and hands it to me.

"You should find all the information you need about the Church of England in there and the days we perform marriages; yes, we only do them between 8am and 6pm on any given day. And there is some extra info thrown in on local services; food, flowers, etc. in case you need it.

"Which brings me to you again Sarah; since you're a citizen of the U.S. living here on Visa, you and Thomas will need a Superintendent Registrar's Certificate to marry. There's some discussion in the diocese that this will change in future to something more stringent, but for the time being it remains as is, at least through 2011.

"You'll need to contact the local Registrar's Office to report intent to marry. They'll tell you what paperwork is required and what you must bring along. There's a twenty-eight day rule so I wouldn't delay in getting a start on it. Any questions so far?"

I look at Thomas, we both seem to be speechless and turn back to the Vicar.

"Good; I can see you're both a little overwhelmed, so we'll end this for today and meet again next week to plan the ceremony and talk about the services you'll want at the Church. I do need to know one thing; have you chosen a date?"

"We'd like to reserve a day for the second week of December," I announce.

"Any day in particular?" His eyebrows rise as he asks.

"We're flexible sir," Thomas speaks up, "we know it's a very busy month and we just hope you can get us in at all. So if you have an opening, we'll plan around it."

"Very nice of you both, thank-you for understanding my dilemma, as it were. Now let me see..." he turns pages on his calendar and moves his finger over the weeks to one day before he looks up at us over his reading glasses.

"How about Wednesday, the seventh; you have a choice between two and six pm; we've added a late hour to our usual schedule due to the holiday demand," he explains.

"What do you think?" I ask Thomas, "Six pm sounds good to me; candles and soft light, no rush to get out of the Church for the next service?"

"You're right, it makes sense. We'll take that six pm slot, please," he tells the Vicar.

"Six it is and I'll make it official with a request for a deposit." He looks up expectantly and Thomas withdraws his cheque book from his jacket.

As we leave, the Vicar reminds us to get the Registrar's office taken care of as soon as possible.

"See you next week Sir and thank-you very much," I respond.

"You're welcome Sarah, a pleasure to meet you and please call me if you have any questions in the meantime."

My movements about the house at night have been restricted since the near-disaster in the closet two months ago and I'm very careful not to stray too far from areas I'm normally assigned duties in. I miss having the run of the house at night as it was ideal for exploring places normally out of my purview.

I've redirected my search since the shell reference in Regis' letter and on a hunch, keep an eye open for anything that resembles a shell in the house or around Highbridge at-large. The shell letter seal found last October makes me realise its mention in the letter is a clue from the Smith's history.

It occurs to me the house plans might shed some light on any other secret niches. I believe they're still stored in a protective folder in the library, but care will be needed in retrieving them. If I'm caught, it will raise questions and potentially expose what I've been doing. The last thing I want is the ruin of the only good family relationship I've known in life.

"Stephen, are you in here?" I ask as I enter our master suite where his desk sits framed by the arched window above.

"Yes Meg my darling," he walks from the dressing room and looks very dapper in a pinstripe, navy-blue suit, "What is it?"

"There you are; I wanted to see if you're ready for lunch."

He comes to take me in his arms for a moment; "I'm making a trip into London on some business today; go ahead with lunch, I'll get something on the way."

"This is rather unexpected isn't it?" I ask.

He opens a drawer to retrieve some papers and drops them into his brief case.

"Yes, I received a call to meet with one of our investment counselors, so I'm off. It's nothing serious dear, so don't say anything to Thomas. No need to worry, just a quarterly report to go over and I'll bring copies home to review with him later."

"Stephen, you haven't forgotten your agreement with Thomas last month regarding the Estate's finances, have you?"

"No indeed Meg; this isn't anything he need be concerned with." We walk down to the front door together.

"Now I'll be home this evening but don't hold dinner, I may be a little late depending upon the motorway." He gives me a quick hug and a kiss then walks out to his car at the terrace steps.

He's excluding Thomas for a reason I suspicion as I return to my desk. It isn't like him to travel into London these days since retiring. Stephen is still on the Board at Smith Imports, but this isn't their regular meeting date. I decide not to worry needlessly and turn to my desk.

Sarah asked that I plan the wedding reception and I'm more than happy to do so, but have decided to phone her mother to see if she'd like to help. I know she must feel left out, given the distance between St. Thomas and the U.K. and Sarah is their only daughter. I'll use the excuse that we're so busy with the Mill I need some help; hopefully, Gloria won't catch on, but I'll let Sarah know my plan in case her mother questions her.

"Sandlin residence" Pat answers.

"Hi Pat, this is Meg at Highbridge."

"Well Meg. How's it going up there?"

"It's coming along, very busy, that's why I've called. Is your lovely wife at home?"

"She's right here, hold on please." I hear him summoning her.

"Meg?" Gloria answers. "What a nice surprise; everything okay?"

"Yes, of course, everyone's fine. We're extremely busy with the Mill; the holidays are coming up fast and of course the wedding. That's why I wanted to talk with you; if you're up to it, could you do me a very big favor and help plan their reception?"

"Well, of course Meg. You know we're retired – we walk on the beach and eat – our two favorite past times. We'd love to do it for the kids; what do you have in mind?"

"If you could please work with Sarah, get her vision of the reception and ideas for food and decorations; that would go a long way to get it together. I really haven't discussed it with her yet.

"Stephen and I would be thrilled to have the reception here but understand if she wants an outside venue. Does that sound like too much to handle from St. Thomas?" I ask.

"No, we can do that; I'm so thrilled that you called, it'll be fun for us. I'll keep you posted on progress and of course, work with you when it comes to the local caterers, rentals, that sort of thing." Gloria replies.

"Wonderful. Okay, I have to fly, but thank-you for the help, Gloria; you're a life-saver."

"You're certainly welcome Meg, email me if you think of anything else, otherwise we'll be talking soon I'm sure."

"They must really be in high gear up there," Pat says after I hang up.

"Yes, I'm sure they are...," I answer him as a little smile begins.

"What's up?" he asks.

"Meg is worried we'll feel left out of the wedding plans; how typical of the Smith family to think of us down here and make such a nice gesture to include us."

Sarah, do you know any more now than you did? I ask myself as I hang up after speaking with Passport Office. There's nothing simple about the process of staying in this country or getting married. I'm on total overload after listening with full concentration to the agent's voice for the last fifteen minutes. I took notes, but when I look at them now, they're a collection of spaghetti-like scrawls.

If I understood him correctly, I'll be applying to extend my Visa as the 'partner of a person present and settled', or was it for 'indefinite leave to remain'? The catch is that my present Visa is for two years and I can't apply until just twenty-eight days before it expires. I have years to consider switching over to apply for citizenship if I want but, that's something I'll think about later.

There's a test called 'Life in the U.K.' which I must pass prior to applying for the new Visa; hopefully between studying the manual and living here for two years, it won't be a problem. Forms must be brought to the Registrar's office at Leeds along with the requested passport, my biometric residence permit and proof of address.

As to our marriage, Thomas and I must both visit the Leeds office at least 28 days before the wedding so that I can register intent to marry. After the wedding, a Change of Circumstances form with my name change must be delivered to them and then a new biometric residence permit applied for within three months or I'll be fined stiffly.

Drained of all energy, I sit rearranging my notes at the kitchen table for a while. It's apparent that I'm not sure about any of it and this is nothing to fool around with; time to talk to Stephen and consult with his solicitor again who helped me get my visa last year.

I watch my beloved countryside roll by while I ride the train into London. *Stephen, if you had a*

*penny for every mile covered to Smith Imports these past years...*I think playfully.

It was a hard decision to retire last fall, but I've had no regrets. My lovely Meg and Sarah's arrival from the U.S. has made me happier than I've been in years. Add to that the freedom to create something new and fresh, our Copper Swift Mill—it's the topping on my cake.

But I didn't really leave Smith Imports last year I now admit, but stayed on the Board to protect the family name and follow in my father Charles' footprints. Lately though, given the time to do some soul-searching, I realise I'm chained to a long family tradition and may have retained ties entirely to assuage my guilt for leaving.

The Company has enjoyed a prosperous and long life; I feel indebted to the Smith men for the privileges they passed on to me. But after forty years I realise the real price they paid; precious time spent on business rather than at Highbridge and with their families. It's my only regret and I wonder...*did they hide similar regrets later in life, too?*

My father Charles entered the company in 1931 to take over for his father and brought me to work after university in 1970. I later chose not to stay and went out to build my own successful business. When he fell ill and asked me to return, I couldn't refuse and came immediately with Thomas and my wife Irene.

I think of her as she was so long ago when her heart took her before her time and left Thomas without a mother. But the years have sufficiently softened the hard sting of grief and with new life in our family again, I won't make the same mistakes I did before.

This morning I awoke restless, looking forward to this train ride to sign over my shares to their new owner. It's time to end this longtime relationship with the import business and let someone else take it on; a logical decision, good for me and for the Estate's Trust. The profitable sale will stabilize Highbridge and with wise management, make Copper Swift's launch easier on all of us.

I don't feel good about keeping it from Meg this morning, but it was a personal decision only I could make and I didn't want her to bear the weight of its knowledge. When I arrive home, she'll be first to hear what I've been up to and I'll ask her forgiveness.

I'll tell Thomas next and after I give my reasons for the way I've done this, I hope he'll understand.

Chapter Nine – Discoveries

G ood morning Mr. Thomas," Jamie stands on the veranda and greets me as I arrive at the Mill.

"I've really tried to mind my own business," he tells me with a laugh as we stand looking out on the Copper Swift, "But I've heard your discussions at breakfast for months and couldn't stay away any longer." He shuffles his feet a little then continues.

"Hearing you and your father this morning really piqued my curiosity and I had to walk down and take a look for myself; I hope you don't mind?" He glances sideways at me then back out to the Swift.

"Not at all Jamie, you're welcome anytime. Come inside," I invite.

His gaze turns first to the café space then to the front windows where morning sun deepens the rich color of the wood in the walls and in the wide plank floor.

"At the last minute, we decided to add this long serving bar across the kitchen area," I tell him. "I'm not sure where we'll go with it in future, but it has possibilities for additional seating if plans take us further."

"I like it," Jamie replies as he walks into the kitchen. He runs a hand over one of the roomy granite counters then spots the new commercial stove and additional ovens.

"Is this a convection oven, sir?" he asks as he opens one of the recently installed units.

"Yes, our kitchen advisor said it was wise to install two types of ovens but the convection fan can be switched off for various baked goods like bread; the other oven is an electric radiant. We have an all-electric kitchen; no open flames here for fire safety. We've successfully addressed the risk of flash fire due to grain dust with our vacuum system, but there's no such thing as 'being too careful'.

"Good choice, sir and convection ovens are terrific for most baked goods; very even-heating," Jamie replies.

I can tell by his wide-eyed expression, he's excited about the Cafe and it's the reaction I'd hoped to see.

"Are you ready to see the rest?" I ask.

"Yes sir, ready when you are."

We walk upstairs and I basically explain the water wheel, its driveshaft and the various mill stones and rollers that finish the texture of the flour.

"We modeled this after the old traditional craft, but with many modern improvements." I point out the cleaner and conditioner equipment where grain is first filtered then sprinkled with water and allowed to sit before it's ground.

"The best improvements in my mind are the vacuum system and the grinding wheels of manmade material; they're stronger and last longer than the old natural stones.

"We can't compete with the big commercial mills and wouldn't expect to," I tell him. "This is a grist mill for craft flours; high quality, good baking performance and healthy. We'll start off simple with a few variations; whole meal, mixed grain, oat and white then see where it takes us."

"I believe there's adequate demand in our district for the Mill, sir," Jamie says, "there are no others within a hundred miles of here, as you probably already know. Are you considering an internet site?"

"It's in our plans but we need to design one and aren't quite ready yet." I pause for a second then change the subject.

"Speaking of things pending, let's sit down for a few minutes." I lead him to one of the benches along the front wall.

"There's something I want to discuss with you, Jamie; Dad and I were recently talking and he reminded me your sojourn with us will soon be up."

"Yes, in four weeks my tuition loan with your father will be paid in full and it'll be time for me to move on. I'm anxious to go forward in life, but it's hard to think of leaving the area. Your family is second-nature to me now, sir and my own family's just down the road; it will be difficult."

"So you have plans for your next step?" I ask him.

"I've considered a move to London, to try for a position with one of the many top chefs there. And of course, in a few years, I'd like to establish a small restaurant of my own."

"You don't sound convinced; do you have room for another option?" I ask with a smile.

"It depends on what you have in mind sir."

"How would you like to stay here as chief baker for the Mill?" I ask him.

"I hadn't thought about just being a baker...I enjoy cooking too much and would miss it."

"You wouldn't be 'just a baker' forever; we plan to see at least a two-star restaurant here and the Café will afford us a trial run on a smaller scale. You'd introduce some dishes of your choice; perhaps using local produce? And if popularity follows, we'd progress to a larger venue on the Estate, maybe in the old stables? How does that sound?"

"I'm amazed you'd consider me for the position sir."

"I appreciate you're humble Jamie, but we know you well after four years; your work ethics and ability to get along with people, the way you manage tasks on your own, all indicate you'd be very good for our business. We'd love to continue your dream while pursuing ours and think the two would be very good for each other. You'd be in charge of hires and training your staff as needed, within budget, of course."

"When do you need an answer?" he asks.

"I don't need it this instant, but the sooner the better. I'd like to start generating excitement for the Mill with advertising and a website as soon as possible; your picture as head chef would be featured."

"You're kidding?"

"Nope— totally serious; the café' could be Jamie's at the Copper Swift Mill someday; think about it and get back to us."

Before returning to the house, he turns to offer his hand.

"Thank-you for your time this morning sir; I will seriously consider your offer and let you know something by Friday this week."

"You're welcome Jamie and Friday would be fine. Since we may be working here together, just call me Thomas. By the way, I need your position filled at the house, so if you have any suggestions for a replacement, let me know."

"I'll do that. In fact, one of my mates at school lives in the area and might be interested."

I've worked late into evening with some research in the library and decide to stay over at Highbridge in my old room upstairs; no sense driving to the cottage at this hour.

"Staying over my love?" Thom comes around the door to ask.

"Yes, I've lost track of time again," I answer.

"Well, I would love to stay up and entertain you for a while, but I'm up early in the morning." He comes to give me a hug and kiss goodnight.

After he leaves, I turn out my desk lamp and walk to the fireplace to stare into the fire, lower now since Berty laid it for me hours ago. I turn to face the room with its heat at my back.

This library has become as familiar to me as my own cottage over the past year. I began researching the Smith's history here and with the accidental discovery of the space behind the shelves, excitement in the research continues to drive me.

The character of the room is typical of the rest of the manor. Colors in the rows of books stand out against the dark oak paneling around the room and either side of this fireplace. The large library table is at center in the room and has been filled at various times with tax records, history books, and house plans as I work my way back to earlier generations.

Sometimes, I try to imagine who might have sat here generations ago and what they did here. I feel certain that more than one head of the family used this very room as he went about the Estate's business or just came to relax and read on a winter's evening. It feels good to know I've been included in a family of this size with all its history. I switch off the lights and walk upstairs.

The space heater in my old room begins to take away the evening's chill and I put myself wearily to bed.

But somewhere later in a sleepless haze, I realise I've only tossed and turned, sleeping very little. Wedding plans run in and out of my brain, and I'm long overdue for 'lights out' at this point.

I punch my pillow then squint through one raised lid to the green numbers of '3:15' on the bedside clock.

That tears it I think and sit up to the room's darkness; *maybe a glass of warm milk will help.* I drag myself over the edge of the bed, shrug on my robe and retrieve slippers on the way out. The small lamp on the hall's side table lends a welcome soft light as I tread the thick carpeting to the back stairs.

I'm glad to find Jamie leaves the under-cabinet lights on at night and they illuminate my path sufficiently to the cooler. The microwave warms my glass of milk and as a second thought, the last scone left over from tea. Yesterday's neatly folded paper is still on the table and I pull out the comics.

But my favorite strips fail to divert me from wedding thoughts and the fact that I still don't have a dress. Not even Thomas's effort to console me with the facts on his mother's wedding problems has helped.

Wait a minute; a rogue thought causes me to look up from the paper; if the portrait in the dining room is an accurate likeness, Stephen's wife Irene was about my size. And this family saves everything...the last hundred years' worth is in the attic. I put the comics back into the newspaper then grab my plate and glass to take back to my room; this is a long-shot, but it might be a solution.

Back in my room, I change into jeans and sweat shirt then finish off my late-night snack for energy.

I'll need to be as quiet as possible since Emily's room is just down the hall from the attic door. I certainly don't want to wake her after her last experience with the intruder in the coat closet. On the way past her door, I slide a note under, just to make sure she knows I'm here.

The attic door lies at the end of the dimly lit hall, similar to the one from an old scary movie. The hall's length is lined by doors to smaller rooms which previously housed a large house staff.

Lucky I don't get spooked at stuff like this I think with a smile. The door to the attic opens easily and I switch on the lights.

Now, if I remember correctly, Irene's trunks are over here under the eaves. It's plain by the lack of dust that Emily has successfully cleaned and I must remember to compliment her in the morning. What am I talking about, it's four a.m. now.

It does seem longer than a year since Thomas and I were up here searching for historical clues. We shared some of our life experiences with each other that afternoon while we perused the attic's furniture and trunks.

He told me about Lydia; I told him about Brian. I remember the look that crossed his face; not strictly plutonic, but I just ignored it. I was such an idiot back then.

My flashlight shines a beam along the rows of trunks stacked two-high and I read their labels. Halfway down the length of the attic, I find four with Irene's name. My stomach gets a little jittery with excitement and I lay the flashlight on an adjacent desk to shine across the trunks.

The first yields some daytime dresses; the second contains skirts, sweaters and jackets; more for city wear, circa 1960's I'd say. I tuck them back in carefully and go to the third trunk. Formal wear, including a couple of short dinner dresses in black and a beautiful ball gown, are inside. I dutifully replace all then turn to the last trunk which sits up under the angle of the roof.

Remaining hopeful, I lift its lid as high as I can and see that a large white box takes up its full space. To open the lid all the way, I'll need to move the trunk out from under the slant of the roof. I lift its end-strap to test its weight and it doesn't feel too heavy.

There's a wooden bench nearby and I move it in close then pull the trunk off its stack onto the bench. It lands safely with a thump.

I hope no one was disturbed with that I think and pause to listen. What am I doing; I can't hear anything from up here and it's the poor soul in the room below who might be awakened. The harm is done though and I may as well finish this.

The trunk's lid now opens all the way and I'm able to remove the heavy cardboard lid of the box inside. By the light of the flashlight, I peel away layers of tissue and find a gown of French lace and satin. I hold it up to see its flutter sleeves of lace, the bodice is satin lined with more lace overlay and the skirt appears to be flared from the waist. I tremble as I know this is the dress but don't want to take it fully out of the box up here. There's a jaunty little hat with a long lace veil in the box, too.

"Sarah?" I hear Thomas's voice behind me and jump so hard I drop the flashlight.

"Thomas!"

"What on earth are you doing up here at four a.m.?" he asks as he picks up the light.

"Looking for Irene's wedding dress." I feel foolish saying. "How did you find me?"

"Emily heard noises and called me. By the time I arrived, she'd found your note on the floor and avoided a summons to the Constable."

"Oh Thomas, I'm sorry for disturbing everyone, I couldn't sleep thinking about our wedding and finding a dress. I went down to the kitchen for some milk and remembered what you'd said about your mother's custom gown and...well...you know me...full speed ahead."

"Yes, I do know you; have you found it then?" He comes closer to peer into the trunk.

"Yes, it's beautiful Thomas, just like your mother. I'll have to try it on to know for sure, but it looks like a near-perfect fit. Do you think Stephen will give me permission to wear it?"

"Given that he thinks of you as a daughter, he'll have no problem with it, but you should ask to be sure." He stops to look at me for a moment.

"Do you know how beautiful you look at 4 a.m. my darling?"

"You're kidding right? My hair is a tangled mess and I have no makeup on," I joke in embarrassment.

"You're a vision; like some wild-haired spirit floating around our attic and I'm going to capture this spirit right now." He takes the dress out of my hands and drops it back into the box then pulls me against him, his kiss warm and passionate before he releases me.

"Come on, I'll take this." He looks at me with longing and touches my cheek then picks up the box to carry it downstairs. We lock the attic door and see Emily down the hall as she leaves her room.

"Well Miss Sarah, you've been busy today already and had some luck I see." She beams at the sight of the box in Thomas' hands.

"Yes, thank goodness; I'm so sorry for alarming you Ems – I was trying to be quiet, but I shouldn't inflict my insomnia on others."

"Actually, I wasn't as alarmed this time as my last 'adventure', but I did have my cricket bat at the ready after I called Mr. Thomas. Then I found your note and knew what was about."

"I'd hate to be the prowler running into you Ems," Thomas declares and gives her a hug.

When we reach my room, he carries the box in and lays it on the bed.

"I can't take it out with you here," I tell him, "bad luck and all that."

"In that case, I'll just collect my fee and be out of here." He steps closer and his lips are warm and sweet on mine, the perfect end to a raid on the attic for a wedding gown.

"Hello Sarah; I hear we had early morning excitement." Stephen announces as he enters the kitchen with a smile.

"How did you hear about it already?" I ask in surprise.

"My son informed me you had something to ask of me and I 'weaseled' the details out of him. The answer is 'yes'; Irene would be honored if you wore her dress."

"Oh Stephen, thank-you so much," I say and give him a kiss on the cheek.

"Not at all my dear," He exclaims, "Now can we get some breakfast around here?" Jamie responds with a large tray of hotcakes stacked and buttered; sausages, brown and crispy and broiled tomatoes from the garden. Meg comes to join us just in time.

"Sarah, I set up an appointment with our Solicitor in York for you and Thomas," she tells me. "He'll work with you on your Visa and your wedding license."

"Thank-you, Meg. That was another thing keeping me from a good night's sleep. Hopefully, it will all work out fine but I'll feel much better after we meet with him."

She encourages me, "They probably encounter this often Sarah; try not to worry."

I do feel better, especially now that the dress hangs in the closet upstairs.

"Meg, have you heard that I found Irene's wedding dress?"

"Yes I did overhear something about a dress in the attic," she laughs. "You need plenty of coffee this morning after last night's activity."

"Absolutely; second cup right here," I hold it up with a laugh. "Would you help me try on the dress when we've finished here?"

Upstairs, I step into the lace and satin gown and Meg gets me zipped up. We notice the label is from Paris and I'm suitably impressed. I'm also glad the zipper is invisible and that there are no knobby buttons up the back; I've never been fond of that look.

"It's lovely on you Sarah," Meg says admiringly and circles me to see from all sides. "This little riding hat and veil is novel isn't it; do you like it?"

"Let me see," I say and put it on top of my head where it feels a little out of place.

"Like this?" I ask her.

"Here, let me try," she says and places it at an angle to the right side of my head, slightly above my eye. "Sort of sassy, don't you think?" she smiles.

"Yes, it does show spunk," I respond, "The veil is very long though; should we have it shortened?"

"It might be more manageable; make it to correspond to the dress's hemline or just a little past?" Meg suggests.

"Yes, I like that. Are you familiar with the village tailor's work? I won't trust just anyone with Irene's dress."

"Yes, he's extremely competent," Meg answers, "and he does quality work. I'll tag along for moral support if you'd like."

It's a clear day in July and quite warm so I decide to shed my jacket for a work apron. Ms. Emily has asked me to gather some garden flowers for the entryway table; not exactly my normal job description but I told her I'd be happy to do so. There's rarely time to take a stroll on the grounds during daytime but gradually over the years I've been able to explore several outbuildings around the Estate at night.

Three small, four-room cottages, quarters for married, higher level servants in the early years, are long empty. Several utility buildings supported the working farm and were storage for grain, feed, and machinery; one for milk from an earlier dairy herd. Then there's the garage, large enough for four vehicles with a private office upstairs for a previous Estate manager.

The stable is especially nice and built at the same time as Highbridge of the same granite; it's stood solid for the last hundred years. Some of its wooden stalls and trim need refurbishing but otherwise it's in excellent shape without equines at present.

The large greenhouse is set on a granite foundation built freestanding in the garden and presently used to store flower bulbs and grow plants during the winter months. It's a welcoming respite to stroll there when the cold north winds blow, its colorful flowers and herbs grow right through the winter.

John the gardener stores his tools there and I decide to retrieve a pair of pruning shears for Emily's flowers. Most of the wooden beds are empty now for the summer, I find the shears easily.

I turn to leave, but stop first to admire the modest stone fountain at the center of the building. Its sound is very pleasant for anyone who works or tours the place; now, as if new to my eyes, the water falls in streams from the fount and rivets my attention.

Its soothing flow is easy to watch, but in one ribbon of water I see something else and step closer. It's the face of my kindred spirit, with the pleasant smile he wore at our last meeting. I take another step forward but he disappears. Something else directly behind the water's flow now takes my attention; a detail I hadn't noticed before.

I'm struck quiet at its simplicity; here in the stone-based greenhouse and openly in view is a shell mark similar to the letter seal's.

I walk outside to gather the flowers Miss Emily requested and try to appear suitably casual though I feel anything but.

It's clearly time to bring the family into this now and they'll think I'm certifiably balmy if I mention anything about the spirit. I know I wouldn't have come this far without his help, but if I expect to be taken seriously, my ethereal friend will need to remain out of the picture.

Chapter Ten – The Maiden Run

It's an exciting day for Dad and me and we take the Rover down to meet our miller, Edward Scott. He'll put the big, underhand water wheel in motion to take the Mill's equipment on a maiden run; a few 15kg bags of grain will be used for the occasion.

"I'm a little nervous Dad; what if it doesn't work as it should?"

"That's why it's a 'maiden run' Thomas; obviously to find any flaws before we open. Besides, we've had only the best consults involved and I believe we have one of the best millers under our employ as well; have a little faith."

"You're right," I give him credit. "We've done all we can to make this Mill one of the best."

"You've done a great job at getting us here Thomas. I have no complaints, except for that little matter of the wall." He looks at me sideways.

"Thanks Dad and on another note, regarding your decision to sell your stock interest in the business; I know it wasn't easy but I admire the way you handled it. It was your decision and even if you had talked with me beforehand I would have been too uncomfortable to give advice."

"I know," Dad says, "and I can promise, in future, any decisions to be made will be discussed first with the family. I've promised that to Meg and expect you to include Sarah the same way."

"No problem there; she's already laid down the law on making decisions without her." We laugh together.

"Yes, I perceive she's a strong woman Thomas, but one who will love and stand by you. Not many are lucky enough to find such a person.

"Your mother was like that, in case you weren't aware and too young to remember. There were times when I was stubborn and she knew just how to handle it. But she was the first love of my life and I have no regrets other than spending too little time with her; I hope you've learned from my mistakes."

"I've listened well, Dad."

Edward waits for us at the Mill's front door and we follow him into the workroom where the large pit wheel lies half-concealed in the floor and already turns by the water wheel's power.

"I started her up this morning so you could see how all this works," he says clearly over the low-level noise. "You can see the wheel's shaft meets the bevel gears here; they turn its power vertical to this main shaft which goes up to drive our millstones and equipment on the second floor.

"Sometime in the future, we can easily add an electric generator to harness this power and be self-sufficient, probably with some to spare for your house, too."

We're impressed with that fact; an unexpected bonus to help us streamline expenses for the Estate and cut our energy bills.

We follow Edward to the large room in the back where trucks will deliver the grain through two large overhead doors. He points to three upside-down pyramid-shaped vats. "These will clean the grain then send it on its way upstairs by vacuum thru a closed, dustless tube system."

"The grain will pass through magnetic fields from start to finish, preventing any metal reaching the grinders or the end flour product." Edward leads us upstairs to the second floor to see the rest of the process.

"The grain comes from downstairs and enters this series of filters to capture small stones and foreign objects; then it passes to the sieves in this unit. From here, it moves on to the conditioning vat where just the right amount of moisture is added as predetermined. That allows us to capture more of the bran in larger pieces and makes for a more attractive and nutritious whole grain flour. By the way, a small amount of chlorine in the water gives the flour a longer shelf life, too. The grain is allowed to sit for up to twenty-four hours before continuing on to the mill stones for grinding.

"As you can see, there's a science involved to ensure the finished flour contains just the right amount of moisture and gluten and I'll be doing my checks along the line to make sure it does. If it's wrong, you'll have a lot of bakers complaining their baked goods won't rise. It's my job to ensure that never happens and as long as you give me quality grain, I can keep you on the good side of every baker who purchases our products.

"In your case," Edward adds, "the local farmers' co-op will grade and examine the grain for disease and quality which gives you an extra safeguard rather than receiving the grain directly.

"This batch of wheat has been here twenty-four hours and it's ready to begin grinding." He smiles and asks, "You ready?"

"We've been ready – let it go," Dad exclaims.

We watch as the wheat is slowly released to the grinding wheels. In about forty minutes we see the finished product flow into 1.5 kg bags with the Mill's logo on the front and some history on the Copper Swift and Highbridge on the back. Edward hands one to each of us.

"Congratulations gentlemen, you're now in the mill business." We accept the bags just as proudly as if they're filled with gold.

"Really enjoyed your presentation Edward, I'd like to film it sometime soon and use it on our website; think you can handle that?" I ask.

"Thomas, I've done that in the past and would be pleased to do it for Copper Swift; just let me know when, so I can get a haircut."

"It's a deal Edward – have a great day, we'll see you tomorrow." Dad and I take our bags of flour back to the house.

"Jamie," we greet him in the kitchen, "look what we've brought you, our first flour from the Mill."

He comes from the stove and accepts the bags. "Thanks gentlemen, a very nice gift. How about I bake something for dinner in honor of the Mill?"

"If you have time, great, but don't let it set you behind; we're a little late with it," I tell him, but he insists.

"No problem, I've got this. By the way, I'm only going to use one bag; don't you want to preserve one since it's your first product?"

"That's a good idea Jamie, glad you thought of that; sort of like keeping your first pound note for luck," Stephen responds. Jamie gives the remaining bag a place of honor in the middle of a wall shelf near the table.

"How's this?" he asks us.

"Perfect," Stephen tells him, " it will be a source of conversation at dinner."

"Miss Sarah." Jamie greets me with a smile then refocuses his attention on a simmering pot.

It's a few minutes before dinner and the kitchen's delicious smells remind me I'm hungry. Jamie's cooking at the Aga and smells from the oven are wonderful.

"Evening, Jamie," I greet him.

Thomas gives me a kiss, "We took a tour of the Mill today with Edward and it was thrilling to see it operate."

"Oh, I would've loved to have seen it too. When's the next tour?"

"We plan to film one for advertising and the web; you can be the 'beautiful family member witnessing the process' he jokes.

"I'm up for the part," I answer. "You know, visitor tours might be a good idea to include in the website. After we're open, a short clip of our tour groups would make a great 'share' on the social networks."

In a few minutes, Jamie brings a sliced pork roast and garden vegetables to the table, serving it all family-style.

"Jamie, you've outdone yourself again and it smells delicious," Stephen declares as he opens his napkin and puts it into his collar. Meg reaches over to pull it out and put it on his lap; he fusses a little but kisses her hand.

"What's the occasion?" I ask. "This is only a weekday; we must have done something to be rewarded like this."

"Edward presented Dad and me with two bags of our first flour," Thomas answers. "We gave them to Jamie earlier and he's prepared a surprise in honor of the Mill."

"That's right," Jamie says, "those rolls you're buttering right now are made from our very own whole grain flour."

We clap our hands in celebration, all agree the rolls are scrumptious.

"Thank-you ladies and gentlemen," Jamie says, "but I have another announcement if I may, while you continue your meal."

"By all means my boy, carry on," Stephen says as he butters another roll.

"Last week, Thomas presented a generous business proposition to me and I've weighed all the pros and cons," he pauses then says, "I've decided to accept his offer of employment as the Mill's baker and future chef of Jamie's at Copper Swift."

"Alright!" I get up and give him a hug. "No one deserves it more than you Jamie; congratulations." Thomas comes to shake his hand as well and fakes a nervous sigh of relief as he wipes imaginary sweat off his brow.

"You had me worried there for a minute when you hesitated. Welcome Jamie."

I can tell Jamie's a little embarrassed but proud at the same time. He thanks us then urges us all to sit down before our food gets cold.

I glance at Stephen who gives one of his famous winks. *Good work Stephen*, I think, you've taken a plain country boy and given him the opportunity of a lifetime.

"Hello darling, are you almost ready?" Thomas asks as he rounds the door of the library.

Highbridge is abuzz today with the Copper Swift Mill's grand opening and I'm here early to help Stephen, Thomas and Meg with the event.

Since the maiden run, things picked up momentum quickly and we've been in a whirlwind of preparation ever since. The website is up and security will keep the expected crowd within the boundaries of designated parking.

Edward worked hard to produce an inventory of flour for display and purchase at the Café's register; popular-sized, 1.5 kg packages for household baking are available in three different types; whole meal, mixed grain, and white. Larger bags can be ordered, though we don't expect much demand today.

A hundred other details have been covered by Emily, Meg and me along with the men. We managed to keep Stephen and Thom somewhat calm despite their tendency to enlarge the least little 'bump' into full-scale doom and we've all arrived at the day safe and sound with a minimum of insanity; *that's equivalent to a 'little crazy', which we all are at this point* I think with a smile.

"We don't want to be late for our own grand opening," Thom reminds me.

"Yes, I'm ready, are you driving down?" I ask.

"I have the 'nelly' outside. I thought it'd be easier than parking a car down there."

"Good idea. I've worn my practical shoes for plenty of walking," I tell him.

Jamie has been instrumental in getting the Mill's kitchen ready and will oversee baking onsite for tour guests. In fact, he began at three this morning in order to have a nice display case full of yummy treats made from our flour for those with a sweet tooth.

He used his local contacts from the culinary school in Manchester and hired two assistants plus a cashier. One of the assistants, Chris Owens, has been hired to fill the position at Highbridge as house chef when he isn't working with Jamie on special occasions.

Thom and I stand a moment in the driveway to look down at the Mill. A few people are already parked and stroll up to the terrace while others have gathered at the waterside rails on the patio to watch the wheel turn.

"It's a beautiful sight Thomas, you must be very proud."

"I am...nervous, but proud; let's go." He's impatient and we climb into the open-top utility vehicle.

Stephen has already set up a table on the terrace to meet and greet guests; both he and Meg hand out pamphlets with information on the Mill as we arrive.

We hear him say to a young couple, "Hello there, glad you could make it. Please feel free to wander at will. You'll find a Café inside and our baker, Jamie, has some nice treats made from our best flour. I believe he has some refreshments available too, so enjoy." Meg sees us and motions us over.

"Stephen, love your welcome spiel; do either of you need a break?" I ask. "Meg, I can spell you, if you like."

"Maybe in a little while; I'm fine for now," she says cheerfully.

"Thomas, better get inside and help Edward and Jamie," Stephen suggests then turns to a new couple approaching him. "Hello there."

Inside we find several people enjoying the rustic décor and the enlarged photos of the Mill's construction that hang around the room. Thomas joins Joe McHugh to mingle and answer questions while I make my way over to Jamie and the new cashier who takes orders at the counter.

"Anything I can do Jamie?"

"Hello Sarah, yes; if you could help restock the display case, that'd be a big help. Chris and Alfred are in the back; they'll set you up with a tray."

"Will-do," I answer. Tables inside are full as visitors sit eating and quite a few have gone to the outside tables.

I stop to introduce myself to several and ask how they like what they're eating; 'delicious', 'super', and 'wonderful' seem to be the words of the day and I thank them before moving on to the kitchen.

"Jamie, do you have espresso?" Edward comes to the Café's counter; it's the first I've seen him stop all day as he's been doing tours for visitors who signed up and there were plenty who did.

"I'm whipped. I must have travelled those stairs for miles today," he says.

"You know, we don't have espresso, but that's a good idea for the future. Meanwhile, how about a strong cup of tea?" I ask. "It's about that time."

"Sold, I'll be over here with my shoes off." He motions to an empty table.

We've finally simmered down in the kitchen and my assistants are cleaning up, so I bring the tea with a scone and fruit spread back to him.

"Thanks Jamie," he says and helps himself to the spread.

"How'd the tours go?" I sit down for a moment. "Did people like what they saw?"

"They seemed impressed for the most part. I did have another miller from a town west of London come up to me. He introduced himself and acted a little cool about our small operation, but I think he was trying hard not to be impressed," Ed jokes as he takes a bite of the scone then puts more spread on its remainder.

"What did you do?" I ask.

"I welcomed him like any of the others; he was really interested in the sieving equipment we bought in Denmark, so that tells me we can't be all that underwhelming," he laughs and takes a long draught from his cup.

"How about you, Jamie, people seemed over the top about your baked goods."

"We filled the display case five times in three hours; I'd say they loved all of it," Sarah answers for me as she joins us.

"We couldn't keep it coming fast enough," I reply. "I knew when they walked in and smelled the aroma from the oven, we'd have them."

"Who can resist that smell—certainly not me," Ed concludes.

"We sold most of the flour this afternoon, too," I tell him.

"You're kidding Jamie;" Ed replies, "that was over two hundred kilos of flour; impressive." He finishes off his scone then asks, "Got any more of these?"

"Good night Mr. Stephen," Chris says to me as he passes on his way out, "see you in the morning."

"Good night, see you bright and early – on time and in the kitchen," I call to him. Can't let the new chef get lax, I chuckle to myself.

Our last visitor left a few minutes ago and the security crew knows we're closed for the evening. I stand on the terrace and look inside at the now almost-empty Cafe where Joe and his wife Dorothy sit with Sarah and Thomas. Edward already left for home and Jamie's in the kitchen finishing up.

The cheery light from the Cafe shines from its windows onto the stone of the terrace where I stand and I can hear the Copper Swift run noisily on its journey past. Its sound reminds me we wouldn't have any of this were it not for the Swift and I say a little prayer of thanks for all; river, family and friends.

"Dad" Thomas taps on the window at me and motions me in. I oblige him and soon take a seat with them all.

"Well Dad, we did it. It went off quite well, don't you think?"

"Couldn't have gone better and I'm pleased as can be," I reply.

Joe speaks up, "We were thrilled that so many came and their comments were wonderful. I think you're going to be very successful here Stephen."

"Thank-you, I hope you're right, I do have a good feeling about it," I tell them and add, "Edward was definitely in his element, eh? People loved his tour, poor man couldn't get a break; went home to soak his feet." We laugh, but it sets me thinking.

"What do you think of setting up an apprenticeship program for youngsters in the area who'd like to learn the trade?" I ask.

"Hadn't thought of it Dad, but it could work; might even cut our expenses during their training; course, it's up to Edward and whether he can take it on and run the Mill, too."

"That's true and I certainly don't want to see our quality suffer. Let's talk to him tomorrow and see what he thinks. I just want to make certain we have backup for him, should he come down with a cold or need time off. Everyone needs it at some point and we should be prepared; having apprentices available would help keep the Mill running in his absence."

"You're right Dad, but for now, I'm beat. I'm going back to the house, have a brandy and hit the sack. Today was wonderful everyone – thanks for all your work."

Joe and his wife add their good nights and Sarah is next.

"Yes, I'm right behind you," she says. "Good night Stephen."

"Goodnight my dear."

After they leave, I walk outside but happen to glance back and see Jamie standing at one of the windows. He raises his hand in a signal of goodnight and I raise my thumb and point to him before I turn to drive up to Highbridge and my Megs.

"Brandy in the great room, Sarah?" Thomas suggests as I come from the kitchen.

"Thomas, I seem to remember another 'brandy occasion' that didn't improve my health the following morning." He knows I refer to last year's celebration after we found the secret shelf in the library. It was the first time I'd had brandy and the last.

"Okay, how about a glass of sherry?" he changes the offer.

"How about that Mr. Smith, it sounds better." We sit on the couch in the great room and watch the fire Berty laid earlier; its flames take the chill off the August evening and hold our attention.

There's a peace on the house tonight, everyone is exhausted from the day's activity and most have gone to bed. Berty will make sure everything is locked up and fires contained before he leaves for his house. Emily is already upstairs after making sure all is in order for tomorrow.

"Could it have been any better Thomas?" I ask him, knowing what his answer will be.

"Couldn't," he says, "Dad wants to start an apprentice program for millers."

"Really? That's so him, always looking for ways to bring new opportunities." I snuggle down into the couch beside Thom and lean my head on his shoulder.

"It is, but I worry this will all become a lot more than he needs at this point in his life. We're going to discuss it tomorrow with Edward and see what he thinks."

"It's a good idea Thomas; let your father present it to Ed and talk it out," I suggest.

"You're probably right; it's his idea and he has a right to work on it." He puts his arm around me and we watch the flames until they begin to die down.

"I really have to get some sleep," I yawn and leave my comfy spot, "I'm turning in." I give him a good night kiss and start to leave, but he pulls me back to continue the kiss a little longer. When we finally stop he looks at me with a smile, "That's to sleep on."

Chapter Eleven – At Last a Wedding

The high ceiling and arches of the Church soar over all, creating a haven of peace and tranquility as they have for more than two hundred years. I quickly go to the small room set aside off the portico to finish dressing but steal a look down the nave as I pass.

It's softly lit by chandeliers and the entire edifice glows. Single candelabra are alight at the end of each pew and decorated with orchids, white stephanotis and satin ribbons. The flowers' spicy scent drifts on the air and I see a few guests already in their seats while the string quartet sets up.

Mom, Meg and I reach the dressing room and I set down my makeup bag on a little table then turn to the full-length mirror. Mom watches as I survey my reflection.

"You look so beautiful Sarah." She dabs her eyes with a tissue.

"Please, Mom, don't cry or you'll set me off and all this lovely eye makeup will slide down my cheeks. And you wouldn't want that, would you?" I try humor as I attempt to get a grip on my own emotions. I'm somewhat giddy inside, anxious to see Thomas waiting for me at the altar, but at the same time near tears at the importance of this day.

Meg comes to her side to pat her on the back. "Now remember, this is a happy day Gloria," she says and Mom seems to get a grip, at least for a few moments.

I turn again to face the mirror and barely recognize myself; who is this dressed in French lace and satin, hair gathered back in a pouf? I can never get this look by myself; there's nothing for it, I'll need a hairdresser on call for the rest of my life.

The lace veil, shortened to a 'mere' six feet from its original ten, is anchored at the back of the vintage hat I found with the dress. Worn slightly off-center and to the right as Meg suggested, it does look rather good. The extra lace around the crown is scattered with small sprigs of baby's breath to soften the look, but this hat is the only detail that still makes me a little nervous.

"Do I appear an equestrian ready to mount my horse?" I ask Mom. It effectively pulls her out of her tearful state to giggle.

"Sarah, what a thing to say; not at all," she scolds, "I love the hat. It's very appropriate for the dress's era, I would tell you if wasn't, don't you agree Meg?" she asks for backup.

"Oh yes, I love the look and Thomas will, too."

There's a light knock at the door and Meg goes to answer it.

"Yes, I'll give it to her." She brings me a notepaper folded in half; "It's from Thomas." I go to the window to read in the multi-colored light of its stained glass.

My darling Sarah, don't keep me waiting any longer, we're meant to be together and I love you so much. Always My Love - Thomas

I refold it and slip it into my dress over my heart.

"Are you alright dear?" Mom asks.

"Yes, wonderful. Thomas sent me a note to tell me he loves me."

"Oh...that is so sweet." She looks on the verge of another tearful episode, but Meg comes to put an arm around her shoulders.

"Gloria, I believe Pat is outside to take you to your seat."

"Yes, of course." Mom gets a grip and throws her shoulders back to stand up straighter.

"I'm so happy for you, dear— love you," she adds and lightly kisses my cheek before she opens the door. I see Dad greet her and she leans on his shoulder as the door closes again.

A few moments later, the music changes to J. Clark's Trumpet Voluntary, our signal that it's time.

Meg hands me my bridal bouquet and stands still for a moment to let me breathe.

"Ready?" she asks.

"Absolutely Meg; thank-you for all your help and for being my Matron of Honor." We share a quick hug then she opens the door. Dad has returned and waits for me with an outstretched hand as Meg passes by.

"You're beautiful my little princess." He hasn't said that to me in years and it very nearly cracks my composure. But he tucks my arm under his and pats my hand.

"You're gonna knock-em dead, kiddo; be happy," he says and it's enough to pull me back into the moment.

"Thanks Dad." I smile at him. We linger a bit to look at each other then take our first steps down the nave to my Thomas.

I see Sarah search for me as she and her father start their walk down the nave together. She latches onto my gaze and never looks away, except as she passes Stephen and Gloria.

Now she flashes me a smile that could light up the world and I can't look away. I know true joy has never been mine until this day and a quick prayer of thanks escapes me for the way she's come into my life.

In just a few moments, her father kisses her and leaves her beside me. We smile at each other again then focus on the Vicar as he welcomes the guests and reminds them of the solemnity of the service. With the proper responses to him, he proceeds to lead us through our vows. We place the rings on each other's fingers and respond to his blessing upon our union.

Sarah waits for me and I take her into my arms. We kiss in front of the filled sanctuary of friends and family as they encourage our effort with applause and a few hoots from the back of the Church. Guess that's what I get for inviting my old university chums but Sarah's lips make all of it fade away for moment until we remember where we are.

After a smile for each other only, we at last turn to face our guests and begin our walk into the world together.

"Miss Emily?" Berty calls me from the hallway.

"Over here Berty," I answer from the corner of the great room as I check to make sure all is in order for the children who will attend with their parents.

I look over the reception tables set up last night to make sure all is ready for the guests when they come. I know Mr. and Mrs. Smith are depending upon me, though we've enlisted Jamie and our new chef Chris to prepare the wedding dinner; the two new assistants for the Café are on hand to serve drinks and hors d'oeuvres. I have extra help with housekeeping chores and Berty can take up any slack, too, if needed.

"Is there anything you'd like me to do at this point?" he asks.

"Actually, we're in good shape. You might keep an eye out at the front door for early arrivals or the bridal couple. Give me a call on my cell should either appear and I'll let Jamie know we'll start with the refreshments."

"Yes mam." He hesitates then inquires, "Are you alright after your scare in the closet?"

I'm surprised he's asked with all that's going on, but I make time to answer his concern.

"Yes, I'm fine. I decided it was ridiculous to let fear get the best of me and I sleep quite well with Thomas's old cricket bat beside me at night. It could level out any threat facing me, don't you think?" I say lightly.

"Yes mam, I believe it might and I'm glad you're doing well."

"Let's get on with it then Mr. Berty and thank-you for asking."

"Very well mam."

I watch him thoughtfully as he walks out toward the front door then get on with my own duties.

The reception and dinner for the new couple were very enjoyable this evening but now Meg and I withdraw to our bedroom; it's been a long day for both of us.

Pat and Gloria are staying the week through Christmas and we have them settled in Sarah's room here at Highbridge. They were set to take a hotel room, but Meg and I truly enjoy their company and wouldn't hear of it.

"We have a big, practically empty house here and what would be the sense in your going to a hotel?" We told them. Since Thomas and Sarah have postponed their honeymoon trip until after Christmas, they seconded our suggestion before they left for the cottage.

"The wedding was lovely, wasn't it dear?" Meg asks me in the middle of my reflections.

"Yes it went off well. Thomas's friend Donnie Ferguson was a little over-enthusiastic in Church with his hoots, don't you think?"

"I think 'hooting' was just fine for the occasion," Meg replies from her pillow beside me, "I wish I could let loose like that sometimes." She smiles and I reach to turn off the lamp. We lie quiet for a little while in the big old house, the fire still crackles and the room is cool, but comfortable.

I take her in my arms where she fits perfectly and we settle into our normal go-to-sleep position.

"Good night, my love," she says.

"Good night, my dear," I answer.

Thomas takes his shower as I sit at my dressing table and brush my hair. I'm amazed at the difference a wedding can make. Suddenly, all is different between us though I didn't think it would be.

We seem to tread more carefully now than before the wedding; we're awkward with each other as we go about our own individual habits of dressing and bathroom use. We even move around the room more carefully in order to be polite. It's clear that though we've known one another for almost a year, we must now learn to be comfortable together in close quarters.

Then there's the obvious barrier removed to our making love after months of abstinence. For my part, I want his passion but I don't know what to expect. I hope it's easy and uncontrived; slow and full of feeling so that I'll always remember this night. I'm a little apprehensive that he may not feel the same or like some, be carried away and out of control. I wonder nervously what he's expecting from me since I don't imagine myself a great temptress.

Brian was my first surrender; we were sort of the ideal couple to begin a new life together, very naïve, young and both virgins. With age comes caution, I suppose; I have perspective on the first decades of my life and they passed quickly; I wish for perfection in this next chapter.

Thomas comes from the shower wrapped in a towel then sees me sitting here and stops.

"I'm sorry, I should have put on a robe but honestly, I have no idea where it is, though I did pack it."

"It's perfectly fine Thom; you should be as much at ease here as in your old room—really," I say to convince him and myself. "All your things are in that closet."

"Good, I hoped you'd say that." He smiles at me then looks in the closet and finds his pajamas where I hung them. I watch in surprise as he drops his towel and pulls on his pajama bottoms. Nice butt I observe and stifle a smile but apparently not too well as he turns.

"What?" he asks.

"Nothing—nothing at all," I say and get up to ask, "Are you hungry? I could go down and make us a snack, if you like." It's a small bedroom and as I move toward the door, he's crossing to the nightstand at the same time.

"Sorry" I say and step aside, but he does the same and we both stop in our tracks to stare into each other's eyes.

"Don't run away from me, Sarah," he says and it's the most natural thing in the world to be drawn into his arms and share his warmth. He kisses me gently at first, but I return for more.

Let's see, what was that I worried about...I can't remember I think as I'm swirled away to some distant space and time. It's a place we seem to be very good at taking each other to and we tenderly promise to practice until we get it right.

Chapter Twelve – Christmas

J amie, are you still here?"

"Back here, Stephen," I call from the kitchen where I've just logged in the cooler's temperature in preparation to close up the Café for the holiday.

Snow isn't expected tonight for Christmas Eve per the weather channel, but personally I'd like some snowfall by midnight and a cover of white by tomorrow morning. I can do for a couple of days with the shovel, but perfection would be a melt right after Boxing Day.

"I've just shut everything down," I say as I walk out to meet him.

"Ah, there you are; good morning." He's wrapped up in a parka with a scarf at his throat. "It's getting cold out;" He exclaims, "some kind of front off the North Sea coming in tonight. You'll be at the house for the festivities?"

"Yes Sir; wouldn't miss it." This will be my first time as a guest, not 'the chef' at one of the Smith parties; *I hope I don't appear awkward at it* I think.

"Good," Stephen exclaims, "I want you to feel like one of the family and enjoy yourself; bring someone if you like, perhaps your parents or a friend?"

"Thank-you but it will just be me tonight. Anything I can assist with?"

"All is taken care of. Chris talked over the menu with Meg and Sarah and he has some surprises lined up I understand. I don't ask and they're not telling so it should be interesting, eh? Alright then, Edward has gone home and you should do the same. Shut the Mill up and we'll see you around six."

"Thank-you Sir, I'll be there." He leaves with a slam of the door after the wind catches it and blows a cold draft through the room.

Unusual weather for this time of year, but thankfully we've no place far to go. Half the village will be at Highbridge tonight; Sarah's parents stayed on after the wedding and Thomas's friend Donnie is already back down with his family from Aberdeen; should be a lively crowd.

I put on my jacket but pause a few minutes to take a good, long look at the Mill's interior.

It already feels like the Café is personally mine and they've given me free rein to begin building a dinner clientele come the New Year. Jamie's at Copper Swift will be on its way and I can't wait to begin my career.

Thomas and I arrive early at Highbridge to help with preparations for tonight's celebration. I'm surprised to see Mom and Dad in the great room helping Em and Berty finish out the top of the tree.

"Hello," we call out as we take off our coats at the hallway closet.

"Sarah, Thomas, good. You can lend a hand with all this." Mom indicates the boxes of decorations all over the couches and still to be hung, but pauses to give each of us a hug.

"Your faces are cold, is the temperature dropping that much?" she asks in surprise.

"It is and I haven't had a chance to look at the weather yet," Thomas tells her, "but if this is any indication, we're in for a freeze tonight."

"I thought I heard you two," Meg says from the balcony rail on the second floor. "I'm glad you're here early. Sarah, may I see you for a minute?"

"Sure, I'll be right up," I answer. Thomas gives me a kiss as if I'm off to the Siberian Steppes, but I'm willing and we linger. When we part, I catch Ems and Berty, Mom and Dad looking at us with sappy looks on their faces.

"Haven't you ever seen newlyweds before?" I ask and they laugh as Thomas blushes a little then goes to help with the tree.

"What can I do for you Megs?" She leads me into her bedroom and closes the door.

"I bought the gift you directed me to purchase for Thomas." She gives me a wrapped present complete with a bow.

"Oh Meg, thank-you for the wrap, it looks lovely. Do you think he'll like it?"

"How could he not; course, you took a chance by not discussing it with him. You can always exchange it, but I think he'll love it," she finishes. "I can't wait to see the look on his face tomorrow."

"Nor can I; we sort of talked about this last year, but he's forgotten all about it by now. It was so generous of Mom and Dad to gift us our honeymoon. Can you sneak the box under the tree for me; I'm afraid he'll be curious if he sees me do it."

"Of course, now go on down there before he gets suspicious." Meg smiles widely before shooing me out the door.

Berty performs his annual reach from the second floor railing to put the star on top of the mammoth tree as I descend the stairway.

"Thank heaven there's a second floor hallway with a railing," Mom says as I approach. "I have no idea how they'd get the star up there without it."

Father whispers discreetly, "Oh, I don't know, maybe put it on before erecting the tree?" She looks up at him and it dawns on her; "Oh you're so smart my dear."

"Comes from experience, I guess." He glances up to see she's directly under the mistletoe and quickly takes advantage to grab a quick kiss.

"Now who's acting like newlyweds?" I ask.

"Okay, point well taken," Pat says as Gloria beams.

The tree looks more spectacular than last year as Emily bustles around its base directing Berty's work up above.

"It's lovely Ems. Are those lights new since last year?"

"The icicles; yes, they're the latest thing and I couldn't decide on pale blue or white at first. But the blue is wonderful don't you think?

"Yes; it really brings the tree to life." The various sized spears hang from the tips of the branches and their soft light travels from base to tip like water drips on a real icicle.

"Are you asking for help from the guests again this year?" I ask.

"Yes, it's a tradition they seem to expect and I seldom have to ask. Just leave the lower limbs bare and put the remaining decorations beside the tree so they can go at it," she answers.

John and his garden crew brought several loads of greenery from the forest yesterday in a big trailer pulled by the garden tractor. The crew decorated Highbridge's gate and its terrace rails under John's watchful eyes.

Berty decked the high railings upstairs around the perimeter of the great room and choice boughs were placed on the fireplace mantels and tables, under Emily's direction.

"Would you mind taking a look at the dining room with me, Ms. Sarah and tell me if it needs anything?" Emily asks.

I follow her in and see she's exercised her usual creativity. The main table stretches its full forty feet; various crystal candelabra are grouped down its center, surrounded by fir and leafy herbs from the greenhouse, the fragrance of basil and pine has increased with the warmer air inside the house.

Fairy lights, tinsel, and vintage glass balls are tucked into the greenery, making both the adult and children's' tables sparkle. I remember how breathtaking it was last year when the chandeliers were turned down and the table lights took center stage.

At the children's table, various stuffed animals; teddy bears, tigers and the like march down its center, at Stephen's request. There are crackers at every place and they'll create quite a stir when the children pull them. I have a feeling Stephen is more child inside than anyone at Christmas as he always adds his own touch to the preparations.

"Beautiful Emily, it doesn't need a thing," I tell her.

"Thank-you Miss, I mean Mrs. Smith," she stutters.

"It's okay; I'm not used to it either. Do you know that's the first time I've heard my new name? Thank-you Emily—I rather like it" We share a laugh then she charges off to check in with Chef Chris.

I look for Thomas and find him in the big chair by the library window. Though it's still light outside, the sky is full of clouds and the breeze continues to push the trees this way and that, their last remaining leaves roll helter-skelter across the yards below.

"It's strange weather for Christmas Eve," Thomas says and pulls me down to his lap. "Great weather for staying on the couch in front of a warm fire," he smiles and adds, "with you."

"Mmm, that sounds good to me Mr. Smith," I confirm and settle against him. We watch the wind take the yard at will for a while.

"Here you two are," Stephen declares. "Have you noticed the time? Five o'clock; we have guests coming in under an hour."

"Oh good grief!" I declare and jump out of Thomas's arms. "I have to get dressed."

"Sorry to interrupt that cozy scene my boy," Stephen says after Sarah leaves.

"No, I'm glad you did Dad, we lost all track of time here."

"Easy to do that with someone you love, eh?" he asks.

"Yes, very easy."

"Everything going well with you two?" he looks at me.

"Wonderfully well, I couldn't ask for more. She's easy to live with, almost too willing to spoil me; I'm in danger of being a contented husband."

"Not an ill-fate my boy," he laughs.

I share his laugh and agree, "Not at all."

The evening's weather turns even colder and guests arrive in their heavy coats. Thomas and I join Stephen and Meg in the front entry to greet them. Berty's on hand to hang coats before taking them through the double doors to the great room where hors d'oeuvres and drinks are being served.

Most go to choose a decoration to hang on the tree as they've done in years past and their talk is amiable, lively even, while they sip their favorite beverages.

The children are especially excited to see the tree lights and the games at the end of the room just for them.

At half past seven, Stephen and Meg stand before the tree.

"May I have your attention?" Stephen asks above the noise.

"Welcome everyone and thank-you for joining us on this chilly evening. It's always warmer where good friends and family gather and we're happy to see you. Now I'm told by Chef Chris that dinner is ready to be served and he would be pleased if we'd come to the dining room. I don't know about you, but I'm more than ready, so follow me!" He smiles eagerly and leads the way with Meg.

We hear 'ooh's' and 'ah's' from the people ahead of us as they enter the dining room; Thomas and I second their reactions as we enter, too. The chandeliers are dimmed and the fairy lights and candles on the tables create a wonderland of sparkling light while the greenery's scent makes the room smell like an enchanted forest.

When all are seated, Stephen stands to tap his glass and the group quiets.

"My family and I bid you one and all welcome." He raises his glass, "Merry Christmas!" Everyone joins in and Emily tells the children to pull their crackers at the same time. They all laugh at the noise they create and scramble for prizes then return to their seats to put on their paper hats.

"As in every year," Stephen laughs at the children behind him, "there are changes at Highbridge and I'd like to share a few with you before we enjoy a marvelous meal.

"The first is the Copper Swift Mill." Someone starts to clap and the rest join in.

"Built and open for only three months, I'm happy to say it's going splendidly. We hope to continue building our production in the coming year and by all signs, Edward Scott our miller is going to be a very busy man.

"Along with the Mill's production, we have new plans to start a miller's apprentice program where young men and women can learn from one of the best; Edward himself will teach the course. It's a two year program opening this spring, with a certificate and a letter of recommendation for those who complete it satisfactorily. Ed, please stand up so these good people can recognize you."

Edward does so and looks down the table to salute Stephen.

"And that's not all," Stephen continues. "our own local chef, Jamie Sellers, has consented to stay on as the official chef at Jamie's Copper Swift Café'; stand up Jamie." Applause from the guests again, as several have known Jamie since he was born.

"We don't have an opening date for dinner service yet" Jamie says, "but I will be offering some ideas for the menu in January and hope you'll join us and give your opinion on them. I have a good feeling about our success in this venture."

Looking to Stephen he adds, "My thanks to you Stephen and to your family for this wonderful opportunity. I'd like now to propose a toast: To Stephen Smith for his interest in the community and for inspiring our young people to take secondary education and stay here as they begin their adult lives."

After the 'Here, Here" response from guests, Stephen regains his composure and carries on.

"Thank you everyone. Now for the best news of the year, as most of you know, my son Thomas and his lovely fiancée Sarah were married two weeks ago. Let's give them a hand, shall we." Stephen picks up his glass as their applause ends.

"A toast then to Thomas and Sarah; may their lives be forever entwined and their marriage long, happy and blessed."

The sound of clinking glass down the table makes the moment and I squeeze Thomas's hand as he sits beside me.

Stephen finishes with his traditional Christmas wish; "Finally, I remind you of the reason we join together on this night; to honor and acknowledge the birth of Jesus, the son of God. May we never forget His sacrifice and keep His love in our hearts throughout the New Year—Merry Christmas Everyone." His words are repeated down the table as he nods to Berty.

The servers bring warmed, white china plates dressed with vegetables and each guest's choice of three entries; vegetarian, ham, or codfish. The vegetables are artfully arranged; baby carrots and crispy green beans; a serving of tasty garlic mashed potato and a sweet mashed squash piped onto the plates. Crispy bread baked by our new chef Chris with good Copper Swift flour is placed down the table and wine poured with other refreshments at request. The table quiets a little as conversation flows and people enjoy their food then lean back a bit to savor each other's company.

As always, children can wait only so long before getting impatient and Emily, who sits with them, signals Meg that it's time and she whispers the message to Stephen.

"If everyone will please claim their children and gather in the great room, I believe we may have a surprise visitor tonight," he announces.

With all the excitement of the wedding and the Mill, I'd forgotten my Dad's part as Father Christmas last year; he was wonderful and the children loved him. Stephen joked about Pat's return in the role every year, but I didn't remember that until now.

When everyone has gathered in the great room, we become aware of the unmistakable jingle of sleigh bells in the upstairs hall. The children hear it too and pause in their play to listen until they see him coming. He begins to throw candy from his pockets over the railing and calls "Merry Christmas, Ho Ho Ho."

All pandemonium breaks loose as parents stand back and children scramble to gather up the candy. My father is dressed in a red suit with fur at the collar and a plaid cap with a sprig of holly stuck into its fur border. He has a big sack filled with mysterious contents and drags it carefully down the stairs while the children circle around him and move with him to the tree.

"Alright boys and girls, because you've all been so good this year, I've brought a present for each of you to open tonight. But first, you must sit down very quietly in a circle here," he points and the children helped by their parents are seated at last, reasonably quiet though most are giggling with excitement and wave at him.

"Very good; Now, when I call your name, come for your present and take it back to your seat as quickly as possible, okay? When you're back in your seat, I'll call the next child, and so on. Everyone understand? Mom and Dad, you may have to help a little," he says with a wink.

It's like a trip back in time for me to see him thus. He played Santa for me and for his grade school classes after I grew up. He joked last year that he's now an international 'Santa figure'; whatever the title, I can't imagine Christmas without my Dad.

"You okay Sarah?" Thomas whispers. Last year this scene caused me a tear or two when I first saw him dressed as Santa, but this year I'm okay.

"Yes, just fine; I do love seeing him this way."

"Pat really knows his way around a candy cane, I must say," Thomas jokes.

When the children are all taken care of, Pat prepares to leave and tells them, "It's time for me to go now; other children wait for me all over the world and I have miles to fly tonight. Boys and girls be good to your mom and dad," he admonishes. "I'll make sure I stop at your house later on with the rest of your presents."

The children wave goodbye as he climbs the stairs and gives a final wave before disappearing down the second floor hallway. We hear jingle bells begin and fade gradually away; even we adults can imagine him in a sleigh streaking across the night sky pulled by eight tiny reindeer; those of us who believe, that is.

After the excitement of Santa's appearance, we invite the guests to help themselves to the various cookies and little cakes on the sideboard; Chris has been busy baking for weeks. Hot coffee tastes so good right now and provides us time to relax.

The time grows late and those who are parents start to gather up their children for the trip home. We walk to the entryway and open the front doors before saying our goodnights to them, where a surprise awaits us all outside.

The wind has disappeared and we find a light layer of white on the front steps and across the lawns that quietly arrived without fanfare while we were busy inside.

"Wow," Jamie exclaims, "I got my Christmas wish." We laugh with him and put on our coats.

Thomas proposed to me on this night one year ago as we stood together on the terraces of the house. I want to revisit it with him so we leave the others to Meg and Stephen.

Around the side terrace, we stand looking out over the river, the Mill and the fields beyond. Thom had the Mill covered with lights in honor of its first Christmas and it looks like a decorated miniature house from up here.

It's a cloudy night unlike last year when the moon was quarter-lit. But the fairy lights on the railings look just as pretty and the smell of wood smoke mixes with the scent of fir boughs to create a unique smell that will always remind me of Christmas here at Highbridge.

"What are you thinking about Sarah?" Thomas asks as we walk.

"Everything; the long journey we've made in the past twelve months since you asked me to marry you."

"And has it been worth it so far?" he asks.

"Oh yes, Mr. Smith. And you; are you satisfied with me?" I ask.

"Totally, unbelievably, magically, Mrs. Smith."

"Then come give me my Christmas kiss now. My nose is cold and needs warming up."

"That can be arranged." Thomas laughs and wraps me in his warm arms that I love so much.

Thomas and I arrive back at the house around ten this Christmas morning and see through the door that nearly everyone is already at the table. Christmas breakfast is usually a little late to allow for sleeping-in after the night's festivities.

"Ah, the smells are back," I declare as we open the door. "Let me see; bacon, sausage, waffles, some sort of cinnamon bread or sticky buns; I can't stand it!" Thomas laughs at me and takes my coat to hang by the door.

"Yes she can," he says in jest to everyone and they laugh, knowing I do have a healthy appetite at times.

Traditionally the kitchen is packed with everyone from the Estate and any guests who stay over. Very few hours pass when some sort of meal or treat isn't being offered and Stephen gives out a generous bonus to members of staff who stay to assist on holidays. Everyone dresses festively in the colors of the season and it's just a very relaxed and enjoyable time for all.

"Good morning Mom and 'Santa'," I say to my parents. They seem to be enjoying their stay and I'm a little sad they'll be leaving for St. Thomas the day after tomorrow.

"Yes, once again Pat, marvelous performance," Stephen says and everyone agrees.

"Those kids were mesmerized," Donnie says, his wife Dee adds, "it was almost enough to make me wish ours were little again...almost." Everyone laughs as their youngest daughter Aileen, now seventeen says, "Oh Mom." Their oldest son Duncan stayed with some friends for the holidays and we've missed seeing him.

"You must come up to Aberdeen in the spring," Dee says. "Your old room is reserved."

"I do want to come there again now that we have time to stay longer," I tell her. "I didn't get my fill of sightseeing in four hours." Thomas and I went to meet Donnie at the university with the historical documents from the library last year and had little time for sightseeing. His input did help us reconstruct the damaged print and lead us to discover both Daniel and Angus Smith's names, previously unknown in Stephen's family history.

"When are you leaving for Aberdeen?" I ask Donnie. "I'd love to bring you up to speed on our latest discoveries."

"We have some time; how about after this fantastic spread?" he suggests.

"Thomas?" I ask to see if he's willing.

"Certainly, I'd like to hear it all anyway as it's been some time since we reviewed it together. Meet us in the library when we're done here, say about eleven?"

"Perfect," Donnie answers.

When we're all seated at the library's table, I open my laptop to show them the family tree thus-far since research began last year. I point first to its base ancestor, Daniel Smith, Thomas's fifth removed grandfather.

"This is all unconfirmed by birth records from Scotland at this point, but he is the best and most logical candidate. Donnie, you saw his first name last year in the bill of sale signature on a farm in New Zealand; then again on a partnership agreement for a granite quarry in Aberdeenshire. I found a Daniel Smith and Rose Smith on an emigrant ship out of Greenock Scotland in 1847 bound for Dunedin.

"Our friend Ted at Village Antiques found a record of awardees for the New Zealand Service Medal and a Daniel Smith was on it. The part you don't know is, I've found a marriage record between a Daniel Smith and a Philomena Gordon in Aberdeen in 1875. The sale of the New Zealand farm took place before that in 1868, the quarry document was dated 1873 so this could be our Daniel returned to the U.K."

"Good detective work Sarah," Donnie says, "but what about that missing time between Daniel's generation and Charles?"

"Glad you asked; one of the service medals we found in the attic was an India Service medal awarded posthumously in 1936 to a Regis Smith."

"Right last name certainly, but Regis was a popular name in that era," Donnie remarks.

"Yes it was." I hand him the letter from Regis to Angus and watch as he reads it; he looks up with a smile.

"You have connection between this Regis Smith and his father Angus; two at one swoop – impressive!"

"Thank-you, Donnie. Now that we have the name, it makes perfect sense why both Charles' and Stephen's middle names are Regis; he was Charles' father not Angus as we first suspected.

"Lastly," I continue, "my Mom and Dad moved to St. Thomas to retire and she sent me a newspaper article about a Brianna Smith Gordon, wife of Patrick Gordon, both from Aberdeen. They founded an art and photography studio in St. Thomas in the early 1900's; their daughter born in London was named Marie Rose and eventually took over the shop for them."

"With all of this leading us down the path to New Zealand," Thomas says, "it's clear we'll have to go there at some point to keep Sarah's bottled-up curiosity from imploding; you know how driven she is, once she's on a trail."

"Well, she landed you didn't she?" Donnie jokes.

"Oh come on guys, you know I ran away," I defend myself.

"Yes, you ran...for a while," Donnie raises his eyebrows at me.

"Ok, you're right; it was fate and I'm happy that it all came true," I admit to him.

"And on that note, thanks for the update; it's really good to see you two together," Donnie says. "I somehow knew it was going to happen, but Thomas, when you were basically chicken on your visit last year and you, Sarah, went back to America, I almost threw up my hands in frustration on you both. But you finally came to your senses; great wedding by the way."

"Yes, we know you enjoyed it by the disruptive hooting in the back of the Church," Thomas says.

"Hooting...me? It must have been someone else mate." He can't conceal a smile beginning and turns away. "Really have to get on the road now."

We laugh at his hasty retreat and later walk with him and his family to the front door. After waving them off, we return to the great room and fall into one of the couches.

"I'm whipped," I declare.

"Just the quiet in here feels good after the past twenty-four hours of celebration," Thom says. We soak it in, but just as we lapse into a nap, we hear Stephen approach.

"Everyone ready to open presents?" he asks loudly. We push back to consciousness and attempt to look energised.

When Meg, Pat and Gloria join us from upstairs, Thomas and Stephen begin to hand out the gifts. Meg and I open ours first at their urging.

"They went shopping together," I whisper to her as we both receive lovely necklaces, different to be sure, but from the same jeweler.

"Thomas, it's beautiful," I say as I gaze at a simple, square cut aquamarine, one of my favorite stones, set in silver with earrings to match.

"Do you like it?" he asks as he fastens it around my neck.

"I love it, thank-you so much," I tell him and give him a kiss. "Now stay here, because your present is under the tree, too." I retrieve it and sit down beside him.

"This is from my parents and from me."

What is this?" he asks as he hefts the box, "It's awfully light." Gloria and Pat watch him closely.

Inside, he finds tickets to Dunedin International Airport on the South Island of New Zealand and looks over at me, speechless. There are multiple travel pamphlets inside to various cities, too.

"It's our honeymoon, Thomas. Well, say something; do you like it? Are you surprised?" I ask.

"This is wonderful! Dad, look...tickets to New Zealand. We've just been talking about the place with Donnie and now we're going."

Thom gives both my parents a hug then turns back to me. "You..." he points a finger at me, "How did you keep this a secret so long? These tickets are dated a month ago."

"I have my ways and an accomplice, whose name shall remain anonymous," I tease him then wink at Meg.

Chapter Thirteen – A Bridge

Thomas, look at this!" Huge white-capped mountains sit majestic in the distance and the azure blue South Pacific lies below us as the plane swings over the west coast and starts its approach to the other side of the island. He leans over to follow the scenery through the window and we can't take our eyes off our first glimpse of New Zealand.

"Spectacular, isn't it?" he exclaims. "I'm so glad we're finally here. Flying half-way around the world really isn't my thing but I can tell it'll be well worth it."

The fact that it's taken over a day and a half of flying time to arrive, plus stop-overs, is old info to me and I'm on the adrenaline of new discoveries at hand. Thank heavens we took a few days' time between connections rather than trying to make it straight through.

Miami was a welcome visit to the U.S. and Thomas enjoyed the unusual winter weather; a balmy

75 degrees and sunny, so typical in south Florida. We walked together on the beach, ate cracked crab and enjoyed the Latin music. Who knew my Brit husband would be a good 'salsa' man? We practiced until the local hangout closed.

In Los Angeles, we took a trip downtown to the Chinese theatre to see the stars on the sidewalk, another one of my bucket list items. We had fun with it; my hands fit those of Judy Garland's and Thomas's were a good fit for Peter Sellers'; very 'fitting' I think.

The plane circles Dunedin Airport now, waiting to land as we anticipate being free from it. This has been a short flight from Sidney; after a fourteen-hour jump from the U.S., we were so tired we checked into a hotel to stay a few days, spur of the moment. Thom at first balked at the idea, but twelve hours later when we felt human again, he thanked me for being creative. He even took me to the Opera House as a surprise, knowing I'd always wanted to experience it firsthand after seeing it in photos.

The plane finally lands and we clear customs. Our rental car is a snazzy red compact with four doors, perfect "to load my souvenirs easily to the backseat," I reply to Thomas's unspoken question. He groans and rolls his eyes, but he'll find out soon enough I always take things back with me when I travel.

"I'm going to drive today," I inform him as he closes the hatchback.

"Are you sure?" he frowns a little. He's given me left-hand driving lessons at home but I still don't go anywhere but into the village.

"Yes I am," I confirm and take the keys from his hand. "I'll be ok, you'll see."

I figure it's about time I bite the bullet and adjust to the left-side now that I live in the U.K. Maybe by the time I drive three weeks in lighter traffic here, I'll be ready for Yorkshire when we return.

I spot an interesting building and recognise it as the Dunedin Railway station I read about on the plane. Its style is Edwardian baroque and it reminds me of a large gingerbread house. Built with contrasting dark basalt and white limestone from Oamaru, the dark gray and white stones are striking together. I decide to make an unscheduled pull-over to read the signage and take a picture.

"What are you doing?" Thom asks, taking his hand off the front dash now that I'm parked.

"This is what we read about, remember? Look, it's one of the oldest buildings in the city — 1903. They run tourist trains from here, wouldn't that be fun?" I ask in one breath.

"Next time, would you please let me know before turning in somewhere?" he says and I notice his glare aimed at me.

"Sorry, I didn't mean to alarm you. Do you feel unsafe with my driving?"

"Well, no...I just don't make unplanned stops when I'm driving; I guess I need to get used to your style." His face relaxes and he even smiles a little.

"Maybe you do," I can't help saying, "because on vacations, I take full advantage of all opportunities to see the sights." I try not to laugh at him; "But I promise in future, I'll notify my 'copilot' of all rerouting, okay?"

"I'd appreciate that and I'll try not to be so easily upset; guess I'm more tired than I thought," he confesses.

"In that case, I'll make no more stops before the hotel and leave the adventuring for another day."

"Well, now that you say that...did you see that road sign back there? It said something about a beach road."

"Thomas Smith, did you just tell me you actually want to do something unplanned?" I chide him, but begin to turn around. "There's hope for you yet."

We follow the road about two miles until we spy the 'Tunnel Beach' sign. We park and discover it's a short walk to an actual tunnel which leaves out on a sandy beach surrounded by cliffs. There are cautions that it's downhill with some loose footing and visiting at low tide is best, so we decide to come back another day to actually go down the trail.

Thom watches with a smile as I take a picture of the sign, then the view out over the pasture in front of us.

"What are you smiling about?"

"Oh, nothing at all," he responds, "I like sheep, too."

"Well we need something to remember our first day and we'll probably laugh about this picture when we get back," I explain. *Even if they are New Zealand sheep in a farmer's field, they're against a view of the southern Pacific*, I say to myself.

A white stone at the base of the sign catches my attention and I toss it into my bag.

"First souvenir?" He must have seen me.

"Sure is," I smile at him.

"You are priceless, you know," he says and plants a warm kiss on my lips to confirm it.

"I am and don't you forget it sir," I answer back.

The familiar ocean-smell of iodine and salt spray is in the air, though we are far above the shoreline. The fresh air is invigorating, a wake-up for my travel-worn brain and the South Pacific surf rolling in down on the beach makes me even more determined to get to it.

We walk a little way up the road, hands linked; more of the coastline is visible below as it rises to high cliffs and sheep climb close along its rocky edges to graze. *Nothing this big and beautiful on the Atlantic side of Florida* I confirm.

"That was perfect," Thom remarks as we get back into the car. "I'm glad I noticed the sign and you were willing to turn around." He looks over at me, "It felt good to do some walking after our plane trip."

"Yes, it did," I agree and he leans over for another kiss.

"I should listen to you more often," he says, "from here on I'm going to concentrate on being spontaneous."

I laugh at the nonsensical nature of his statement knowing that if you have to think about it, it isn't spontaneous, but there's hope for him.

We find our hotel in the hills above the City's circle. The building is modern, recently built and nicely designed for privacy. With the view of the harbor out our window and a little terrace all our own, we're well satisfied with the accommodations.

"All I want is to unpack and take a hot shower," I say as Thomas arrives with our luggage.

"I'm for that," he says. "We can take a walk downtown afterwards and see what it has to offer in the way of food...and souvenirs." He waits to see if I'll respond.

"Good idea." I ignore the extended bait and set to unpacking our bags.

It's twilight by the time we venture down the sidewalk; per our desk manager, a nearby restaurant serves excellent Italian and French cuisine and we find the place in a late 19th century brick building. It's a time warp experience with a mix of old collectibles and modern lighting. I love eclectic but because we've been inside so much today, we decide to sit on the courtyard outside and enjoy the evening.

"I'll have the French onion soup to start, please," I tell the waitress, "and the chicken breast over arancini."

"French onion soup for me, too," Thom orders, "but I'll have the fish of the day with the spinach polenta."

"What was this building back in the day?" I ask the waitress.

"I believe it was some sort of warehouse but honestly, I don't know for sure. Is there anything else for you?"

"No thank-you, I'm fine," I tell her and smile at Thomas after she leaves.

"Please remind me when we get back home to train our Café staff and make sure each has a working knowledge of the Mill's history so they can answer simple questions about it and the Estate."

"Yes, good idea," he answers. "It's universally common, isn't it; the locals are used to what we tourists consider new and exciting, almost as if they've become immune to it."

While we wait for our drinks, I take a look at the city directory from our hotel. *There has to be a genealogy society here* I think, *but this museum looks intriguing.*

"Thom, look; Otago Museum has a southern land exhibit. We have to go; maybe we'll see something to lead us to Daniel's farm location."

"Good idea and if there's a library, I'd like to check it out, no pun intended. They might have a genealogy center on local families."

Our drinks arrive and Thom makes a toast; "To my beautiful wife; may our combined honeymoon and family history vacation be one of our fondest memories." He raises his glass to mine.

The onion soup is just what it should be; warm, oniony and lots of melted cheese over a bread crust on its top. The rest of the meal is delicious and we finish every bit on our plates. We're surprised when our waitress returns with a small cake.

"I heard you mention you're on your honeymoon and when I told our chef, he asked me to bring this to you." She explains with a smile. "It isn't something we usually keep but once in a while we order it in for birthday parties, that sort of thing. You're a Brit aren't you, sir?"

"Yes, from the Yorkshire area and I do recognize this cake." Thom says. "It's a lolly cake isn't it?"

"Yessir, it's on the house. Have a wonderful stay with us." She smiles and leaves a box for the treat before attending to another guest.

"How nice, have you ever tasted one, Sarah? It's kind of traditional for children's birthdays. Here, it's a lolly pie, but Ems always called it a 'cake'."

"Never have; what's in it?" I ask.

"You don't want to know, probably five-hundred calories per inch," he exclaims with a laugh. "Let me see, I believe hard marshmallows, crumbled biscuits, condensed milk and butter are the main ingredients...oh and it's rolled in coconut."

"Ouch" I exclaim, "a recipe for weight gain and hardening of the arteries; sounds delightful and I can't weight...get it...'weight'...to sample it. But I'm too full right now, maybe later tonight?"

We say goodnight and start the short walk back to our hotel.

"You seem to know a lot about lolly cake – how?" I ask him.

"Ems used to make it for my birthday and she let me help as a young lad. I loved them and haven't had it in years."

"Let's stop for tea at the hotel," I suggest, "I'm just not sleepy yet."

We bring our tea out to a table on the patio and Thom picks at the lolly cake while I pull out my tablet to look up the town's library.

"There's a genealogy section at the local library and also a university library; looks like we have our work cut out for us tomorrow."

"Please try to remember we're on our honeymoon and schedule some time for us, too," Thom chides and reaches to close the tablet's lid.

"You're right of course," I agree and take a bite of cake then get up to stretch my legs and lean on the rail around the edge of the patio to look at the beautiful night sky.

She stands before me at the edge of the patio, the lights of the city before her. She wears a summer dress that leaves her lightly tanned shoulders bare, her auburn hair just brushing them. When we first met, Sarah wore her hair straight, but after a few days of U.K. weather, she had tendrils all around her face and never returned to the drudgery of an iron again; I must admit it is incredibly sexy this way.

I go to put my arm around her lovely shoulders. Full night is upon us with stars bigger and brighter than I ever remember seeing at home. We notice the view of the harbor slightly visible through the landscaping around the patio and move to a higher level to see it better. The lights of the surrounding hills and the red and green running lights of night vessels add to the magical scene below us.

"I love you Sarah," I tell her and gently kiss her neck and nuzzle her ear. She turns to me and kisses me back.

"Why, Thom?" she asks.

"Because you love me enough to put up with my impatience," I admit.

"Then thank-you for putting up with my spur-of-the-moment decisions," she kisses me again.

"I thought you knew," I confess, "that's one of the things I admire in you; I've been boxed-in all my life and it's clear I've needed you to teach me how to be more spontaneous."

"Upstairs?" she asks with a smile.

"Upstairs it is." We kiss once more before we pull away from the lovely scene before us and walk to the elevator; just being spontaneous for a change, I smile as I follow her in.

Thomas and I take a seat at one of the Library's tables and tell the assistant "We're looking for anything on a Daniel Smith family in the mid 1800's. He was an emigrant from Scotland."

Within a few minutes, she returns with several books.

"You may want to query the computer as well," she points to a bank of computers on the other side of the room. "There might be something in the database from other sources, newspapers and the like."

"Thank-you, we'll take a look. Oh and there was another man named Shepherd on a bill of sale for a farm in the area, circa 1868."

"Sales of land in that era were recorded but because of their age, the original documents are stored in the Archives NZ," she tells us.

"The LINZ, that's the Land Information for New Zealand database, could help, too. Since you're not a resident, you'd need a copy of the document and an address to confirm the registration district of the property," she finishes.

"So, is this LINZ in the city?" Thomas asks.

"No," she answers, "there are three offices; Wellington, Christchurch, and Hamilton. If you look up LINZ on your laptop, you'll see all the information and phone numbers."

"We will, thank-you for your help," I tell her.

"You're welcome, just find me if you have any additional questions."

"She's very pleasant" Thom remarks.

"I have a photo of the document stored in my laptop," I tell him, "I hope they don't need the original. Maybe we should arrange a visit at one of the offices while we're here," I tell him.

The librarian brings us six, pretty substantial books about the area in the early 1800's and though quite interesting, there's no way we can read them all and I push some over to Thom.

"Let's split these up to save time; you take these and I'll look up both names in these."

"Yes mam." He salutes me with a smile.

"Sorry, I get a little bossy on the genealogy trail. Love you?" I say meekly.

"Love you," he says and pulls his share of the books closer.

Some don't have indices or a glossary of family names, so I skim through them then copy titles and author in case I want to find them later.

While Thomas finishes up his books, I go to the computer to see if Daniel and Mr. Shepherd are included in any of the library's references. There is one newspaper article dated 1868 and I go to retrieve the assistant for help with the microfiche projector.

The article says a new hall was financed by a donation from a Mr. Ethan Shepherd and a Mr. Daniel Smith at one of the area's churches. Bingo!

"Thomas." I call out without thinking, then remember where I am and motion to him to come quick.

"What is it?" he asks quietly.

"Look at this article; Daniel Smith is mentioned with an Ethan Shepherd; remember that name on the bill of sale for the farm? And this is dated a few months before the sale."

He begins to read through the article, "It says Daniel and Ethan donated a generous amount to build a new meeting room. And it was named after their deceased wives, Rose and Catherine. Do you think it's survived all these years?"

"I don't know but we need to dig further to find out," I tell him.

"More importantly, my 5th removed great grandmother is supposedly buried somewhere here in Dunedin," Thomas says as he points to the screen. "Look for a list of cemeteries, here's the name of the church."

"There's a list of churches on my tablet, but no mention of church cemeteries; I'll check again though." I pause as I think of something else. "It's possible the church didn't survive through the years or was joined with another."

I return to check the Library's computer file but only one church has roots in the area during the time of interest; the High Church of Scotland Presbyterian started out small around 1848, but I see no mention of a graveyard connected with it.

Thomas has finished his share of the books and now stands in front of me. "Are we ready for some lunch?" he asks.

I glance at my phone and it's two o'clock in the afternoon. "I'm sorry Thom; I didn't realise it was this late."

"Yes, I understand; remember the first time I phoned you in the States? You'd skipped lunch and dinner and it was eleven p.m.; even Tom was upset with you and wanted to be fed. Let's go, you're officially on break for at least an hour," my husband says.

We walk out of the library and down the street to a café we noticed on the way in.

"They have hamburgers," I note with surprise. "I'll take mine with a slice of cheese and some crisps, please," I tell the waitress.

"Sounds good," Thomas responds, "I'll have the same. Can you bring us two ales? Thanks." He looks at me, "We made some good progress this morning; what say we go to the museum this afternoon?"

"We should take another hour at the Library, but the museum would be a nice break when we're finished." I open my laptop, "Their website says they have an exhibit on the gold strike in Otago; perfect!"

By closing time at the museum we've finished our first day of research. Instead of celebrating we've stopped for Chinese takeout downtown before returning to the hotel. We're both tired and ready to stay in with the 'telly' tonight. Our room is cozy, the terrace offers fresh air and a beautiful view; what more could we want?

This morning I try to wake my beautiful wife who's still asleep beside me.

"We wanted to get an early start, remember?" I whisper in her ear.

"Husbands who keep wives up late should not whisper in their ears at eight a.m," Sarah says without opening her eyes. But eventually, she opens one eye then another to fully focus on my face.

"How do you do that?" I ask.

"What?"

"Open one eye like that; I can't do it." I prove it by trying and she laughs at my attempts.

We decide to visit the N.Z. Historic Places office to get acquainted with their organisation and see what properties they have in the area. We're surprised to hear they have over forty sites under their wing and all are listed on the National Registry.

"We're visiting on a combined honeymoon and genealogic research trip," I tell the receptionist. "In fact, I married my family's genealogist."

"Well, congratulations to you both," she smiles, "and welcome to our city."

"Thank-you, we've enjoyed our visit so far and have found some information on my fifth-removed grandfather, Daniel Smith. Actually that's why we're here, do you have any information on a farm previously owned by him or by an Ethan Shepherd?"

"I can tell you that the only farm structure we have on the Register in this area is a home moved from its original location in the late 1870's by a James Ferguson. Does that name mean anything to you?" she asks.

I look at Sarah, but she's drawing a blank.

"We have nothing." I answer.

"You may want to visit the place anyway, it's quite interesting. Mr. Ferguson was one of the town's early solicitors in the late 1800's. His thought was to live in the house while preserving it as an example of early farms in this area. It's built of stone and survived quite well. If you'd like to visit, a donation will make you members and you can visit any other Heritage properties in New Zealand."

Sarah is enthusiastic so we pay for membership and receive a pamphlet with a list of all historic places listed by the Foundation.

"I'll just give your name to the current owner and tell them to be expecting you within the next few weeks," the attendant explains.

"Another question, sort of out of your bailiwick I'd imagine," Sarah says. "Where would a person be buried during the 1800's? Did churches have cemeteries at that time, or was there a common cemetery used for all denominations?"

"There are several cemeteries in the area presently; I don't know their origin dates although I could pull some reference books for you to work on." She stops to consider the question for a few seconds. "You know you may get a more timely answer from one of the local funeral services. Most are educated in the history of their trade and it may save you some work.

"Also," she adds, "you could stop at one of our larger cemetery parks, the Southern for instance and speak with their office, they'd know as well."

"Thank-you so much," Sarah replies and we walk back to the car while she glances through the Heritage pamphlet.

"Thom here's the farm she was telling us about, shall we go there next? The address is listed in the south end of the city."

"We have time," I reply and pull up the map on the laptop while she drives. I'm adjusting to Sarah's style of driving and can even look away from the road now. I smile to myself, I suppose I am a tad straight-laced compared to this American.

The highway out into the foothills south of town takes us to farm country with houses surrounded by large fields and trees lining the roads. The green fields are full of grazing sheep and the land beyond them rolls down toward the harbor.

"Look...there...a little stone cottage, maybe that's the one we're looking for. Slow down," I instruct as we near a large farm on the highway with several barns. We both see the sign at the same time.

"Here's the sign, turn here," I direct her.

The little house sits at the end of a gravel lane that runs alongside a big, modern farm and I'm struck by the contrast between the new and old. We make our way slowly down the lane and park in front of the cottage. We both take a moment to look it over before getting out.

Small by today's standards, the stone house is perhaps five by nine meters with two dormer windows on its high slate roof. Its stone walls are bleached almost white by years of New Zealand sun and green-leafed vines grow up to the roof in sharp contrast. There's a sign on the wall next to the door and we leave the car to read it.

I read out-loud "Early Settler Home" then below that, "James Ferguson, Esquire, 1879."

I grab Thom's arm when I see the third and fourth lines of the sign; we both hang on them before saying anything.

"Daniel Smith 1848 to 1868' and look at this!" I point to the final surprise, a painted yellow scallop shell beside the date.

"I wonder if the Heritage society or the owner knows what this shell signifies," Thom says in awe.

I read the last line; "Robert and Mary Riley – 1828–1838. Thomas, this house is at least a hundred eighty years old," I remark to him, "and your grandparents lived here until 1868."

"That so?" We both jump and had no idea someone was behind us.

"Whoa there, it's okay folks, I'm the owner," he says with a smile. "Didn't mean to startle you, I couldn't help but overhear what you just said." He takes off his hat and introduces himself with hand outstretched.

"Harley Ferguson, great, great, great, grandson of James Ferguson," he finishes.

"I'm Thomas Vail Smith and this is my wife Sarah." Mr. Ferguson gives us both hardy handshakes.

"Let me guess;" he says with a grin, "great, great, great, grandson of Daniel's. It's a real privilege to meet you Thomas and you too, mam."

He takes out a key to unlock the door and pushes it open.

"We had the house wired for electricity years ago; makes it simpler during the darker months when people want to visit," he explains. "Come on in. How'd you find us?"

"That's a long story Mr. Ferguson," I tell him with a laugh.

"Call me Harley, mam; after all we're almost kin. Daniel was like an uncle to my grandfather James back in the day. Take your time and look around," he invites as we step inside. "If you have questions, just ask."

I feel we've stepped back in time; the furnishings are mid-1800's right down to the kitchen tools, the fireplace and the handmade rag rug on the hearth; but my eyes keep returning to the little sketch hanging in front of us as we enter; a very pretty woman of about thirty or so with curly red hair and blue eyes.

"That's Rose Smith, Daniel's first wife," Harley says as he follows my line of sight. "Had it reframed a few years ago, museum quality; cost me plenty but didn't want it lost to time and sunlight. If you look at the artist's signature, it was done by one of Daniel's daughters when she was just a young girl."

"Let me guess, Harley," I say, "Briana."

"Ah, sounds like you've been doing your homework Sarah," he laughs.

"Actually my mother and dad moved to St. Thomas and sent me a recent article from the newspaper about Briana Gordon's art studio there in the late 1800's," I tell him. "We've just been very, very lucky in our search."

The narrow stairs in the main room take us up to the loft; beds and dressers are in place, pitchers and basins sit on washstands, hooks for clothing are still on the walls and a cradle sits in a corner. We look out the dormers at the land sloping away down to a stream and imagine what it must have been like in Daniel's day. Thom places his hand on the wall to feel the stone as I watch him and snap a few pictures for our album.

"We should go down," he says at last, "Harley will think we're never leaving."

"Now that's not true," we hear Harley call from downstairs, "but I do have a suggestion."

"What's that?" Thomas asks as we walk down the stairs.

"My wife just laid tea so why don't you two drive back to our house and come on in. We can take our time and you can learn more, that is if you don't need to be somewhere else?"

Thom and I look at each other and know we can't refuse his offer.

"We'd love that Harley," Thom answers, "thanks very much."

I'm fairly jumping with excitement at what we've found and admit it's one of the most bizarre experiences I've had in my life.

"This is just unreal, isn't it" I exclaim to Thom as I start the car.

"An understatement; how could we know when we stopped at the Heritage office we'd find the very place we were looking for?" His eyes widen and he remembers something else, "Harley may know where Rose and Catharine are buried."

Our host has already taken a short-cut across the field in time to open his back door for us.

"Welcome folks, this is my wife, Becky."

"Come in, come in," she says cheerfully. "I'm thrilled to meet you both." The blonde-haired, petite woman stands in direct contrast to Harley's tall and burley appearance.

"Thank-you," Thom says. "We didn't expect to meet someone actually connected to the Smiths on this trip."

"I have hundreds of questions," I add, "but I'll save them until we settle down a bit."

. "That's no problem Sarah; you ask as many questions as you'd like," Becky says and places a tray of sandwiches on the table then brings the tea.

"Your china is so pretty," I tell her. "Staffordshire isn't it?" The pattern is a bouquet of pink roses on green leaves; all pieces are edged with bands of green leaves and gold trim.

"Thank-you; yes, it belonged to my mother. Some people like to put their antiques in a cabinet, but I use mine in honor of the people who gave them to me. My maternal grandmother purchased them in London. Please, help yourselves to the sandwiches;

we don't stand on formality in this house. Would you prefer coffee, Sarah? I notice you're from America."

"Am I that obvious?" I ask with a laugh. "I would love a cup, if it isn't too much trouble."

"Not at all and yes, we get quite a few tourists from all over the States; even have some who've never left. Now tell us how you found us, I'm dying to know. I love genealogy and know this kind of break-through is a thrill," she says as she prepares the coffee.

"It is," I admit, "truth is, we're here on a combined trip. Thom and I were married before Christmas and we waited to take our honeymoon until after the holidays."

"Well, that's wonderful; congratulations," Harley says, "and you decided to combine your honeymoon with genealogy; I don't think I've ever heard of that before," he says with a laugh.

"You just don't know Sarah," Thom laughs with him. "She surprised me with tickets for Christmas; once on the trail, she's a driven researcher."

"It's just good sense," Becky says with a smile, "You wouldn't want to waste all your family clues by not pursuing them while here, would you?" She brings the coffee pot to the table and winks at me.

"No, I wouldn't," Thomas answers. "I'm very much in love with this woman, so just between you and me, she could get tickets to the moon and I'd follow her."

The sandwiches quickly disappear as we listen to stories about Daniel, Rose and their children as well as James Ferguson, his mother Jane and Ethan Shepherd. We're surprised to hear Daniel's daughter Briana had a twin sister, Kenna, who wound up being one of the first woman solicitors in Aberdeen.

"Grandpa James' father was a fisherman from Wellington;" Harley tells us, "he died at sea off Dunedin leaving his wife Jane and son James to fend for themselves.

"James met Daniel and Rose when they first came ashore; he was only twelve and worked his goat cart at the docks, hauling trunks and the like to make extra money for his mother. They became fast friends with Rose and Daniel; it was Rose who eventually introduced Jane to Ethan Shepherd and they wound up marrying not long after."

"Now the newspaper article we found at the library this week," I remember out-loud, "said that Catherine was Ethan's deceased wife so was Jane his second wife?"

"That's right Sarah; Catherine fell off her horse and died of her injury several years before Jane met Ethan," Harley explains.

"We have a signed contract between Ethan, Daniel and a third party," Thom tells him, "but we're unable to read the last signature."

"Probably Thomas MacAndrew; he was the town blacksmith. The three were inseparable through the years, good friends tried and true. You're doubtless aware of the Shell gold mine Thomas?" Harley remarks, "They were all partners in it."

"Why...yes, sort of...," Thom hesitates as he processes what he's just heard and turns to look at me.

I'm amazed that so many questions were just answered with so few words and tell Harley, "We suspicioned early-on that Daniel might have had his start in Aberdeen from a gold find."

"Your suspicions were accurate, Sarah." Harley gets up from the table to approach a nearby cabinet.

Thom adds, "We've seen the shell motif on a letter seal and on a contract found last year; it's been quite a mystery for us."

"This is what you're referring to I believe?" Harley smiles and hands a bag to Thom who withdraws a brass letter seal just like ours.

"It is indeed." Thom holds the identical seal then passes it to me.

"This one was passed down to James from his father, Ethan," Harley explains. "The three partners in the mine each had one to seal correspondence and contracts with." He replaces the seal in the cabinet.

"This is just a small part of his legacy," he continues. "Daniel influenced a whole lot of lives in his time, more than we can probably imagine, beyond our own families. Indirectly, James wound up with his mother's inheritance from her marriage to Ethan and he split it with his half-brother and sister; all enjoyed good solid lives thanks to the partnership Daniel opened up with his friends.

"The church at that time passed on Daniel's financial support to hundreds of early settlers who needed help. Did you know he also left a trust for a native family in the area?"

"We didn't know that," I say in surprise.

Thom asks, "How <u>do</u> you know that?" But Harley is already into the story.

"Daniel and Ethan had what could be described as a 'working agreement' with the local chief during the time. They 'donated' various livestock each year, in exchange for a peaceful coexistence on the land. Daniel in particular became friends with the native and before leaving the country he set up provision for financial assistance to the aging chief's family, administered by Ethan anonymously."

"Do you know where the mine was located?" Thom asks.

"Yes, about three miles from where we are now," Harley replies. "Your grandfather literally picked up alluvial nuggets for near ten years right out of the stream that ran over his property. Today the open mine site that was developed after Daniel left is a lake with homes around it.

"My grandfather James bought the farm when Daniel left for Aberdeen and promised to take care of it for him. The mining company they hired later discovered a new vein of ore under the pasture and was set to dig an excavation that would destroy the house. James took his promise to Daniel very seriously and did what needed to be done to protect it.

"He didn't have enough financial resources, so he approached Ethan Shepherd and Thomas MacAndrew. With their help, he had the house taken apart block by block then moved here and rebuilt by a local stonemason.

"Ethan and Thomas sold their shares in the mine when the first ten year contract was up and retired very comfortably. Daniel renegotiated the mining company's contract with their office in London and rode it out until the mine closed, about twenty years later. I still marvel at the fact that he had the presence of mind to take a chance like that at his age, about sixty-one I estimate." Harley pauses to take a sip of his tea and begins another story.

"Did you know Daniel nearly lost his life while delivering gold ore to the bank? He and Ethan were accosted on the road by a robber who'd monitored their weekly trips into town. He took a shot at Daniel before Ethan could grab his shotgun. Daniel went down, but Ethan made good with his next shot and Daniel lived with only a scar on his forehead to show for it. The fella he shot lived to go to trial in Wellington and both Ethan and Daniel testified."

"Harley, how do you know all this?" Thom asks. "It can't be just word of mouth after this much time has passed."

"My grandfather James kept a journal all his life. It was a hobby for him and he had a sense of how important these stories would be. His children and those that came after made sure his journals were passed down and taken care of. I have to admit, with that many people handling them though, they were in sorry shape when they came to me."

"Yes they were," Becky says, "but I insisted they be reproduced and entered to a computer while the pages were disassembled. We hired a printing company right here in Dunedin so we could work with them; about five years ago wasn't it dear?"

"Yes, and it took some time." Harley reaches into his shirt pocket and pulls out a flash drive.

"It's all on here Thomas; take it home with you." Thom and I look at each other.

"I don't know what to say," Thomas responds as Harley lays the gift in his hand. "I'll never forget this day or the generosity you've both shown us."

"It's all in the family isn't it?" Harley says with a smile. "Though we're not blood, we're close enough to it and I consider us all to be responsible for keeping these stories intact for those who come next. That requires determination from all descendants and friends of descendants. Besides, it's what Daniel and James would want, don't you agree?"

We both smile at Harley and Becky, too impressed by his words to speak at first.

One more question before we call it a night;" Thom says, "do you have any idea where Rose or Catherine might be buried?"

"It's a question we've both tried to answer," Becky says, "but unfortunately, the burials of early settlers weren't always recorded and the cemeteries weren't taken care of in the early years."

"The earliest cemetery on record was moved to the newer Southern Cemetery," Harley explains, "and it's believed many records and remains weren't moved, for whatever reason. I wish I had more to tell you."

"I'm exhausted Thom; after experiencing that much excitement and input, the aftermath is like being in shock isn't it?" We lay in bed and it's near midnight but just can't seem to close our eyes.

"We've learned so much and we have an actual copy of James' journal," Thom remarks, "who knows what we'll find in there."

"You realise it'll take us years to read it all, don't you?" I tell him. "We need to split it up at least between us, maybe Stephen and Meg, too. The more readers the better if you'd like the "rest of the story' before we're too old to appreciate it."

"Speaking of 'too old'; certain facts about my life have become crystal clear with this trip." Thom turns to me and props himself up on one elbow.

"How do you feel about children?"

"I hope you don't mean as of tonight because I'd have to say 'later.' I tell him.

"Ok," he laughs, "but really, what do you think?"

"We discussed this before we were married dear, I love children. They're not exactly something you order off the menu, though." But I see he's serious and let him continue.

"All this talk about heritage and families past makes me realise I'm almost thirty-six and what do I have to show for it; I haven't even started my own family yet. Dad must have given up hope before you came into my life."

"Your biological clock is ticking Thom and yes, Stephen told me he was beginning to wonder," I reveal. "From all I know of him, he'd be over-joyed to be a grandpa, don't you think?"

"He'll spoil our kids rotten for sure; we'll have to keep a close eye on him." Thom laughs then turns serious again. "I'd like to start our family soon, that is, if you're ready."

"I am, darling and a little Vail or Rose would be heaven to me."

Chapter Fourteen -Home to Highbridge

It's the end of our second week in New Zealand and we mark the occasion with a side trip to see the blue penguins at Pukekura.

In the early morning we watch from our perch on the observation platform as the little birds venture from their burrows and walk out across the beach to the southern Pacific. I am totally taken with their color, a lovely, rich blue that makes one want to be close enough to touch them. But they seem happy to be out of reach and go about their routine without the stress of dealing with humans.

The sun does a slow ascent as their day's activity of diving and feeding begins. We're told that sea lions, sharks and leopard seals can attack them at any time and fishing nets are enemies, too.

Unleashed dogs on the beach are banned and their owners receive a hefty fine if they don't comply. All is clear at present though and the little birds move in groups, a small community to a big ocean.

"Thom, the Royal Albatross Centre is just down the road and listen to this;" I say as I read the pamphlet to him while he starts the car. I relax as a passenger for a change and act as tour guide.

"There's a great lookout, a Fort and the Taiaroa Head lighthouse. Can we go there next?"

"Sure, we have nothing else planned, let's go," he says, demonstrating his spontaneity skills which have improved greatly during our stay.

There are so many things to see and do, other than genealogy I admit and we try to do something different each day. We took the Taieri Gorge train tour all the way to Middlemarch last week; the countryside was amazing by a rail route built during the gold rush.

The Gorge itself was impressive, cut deep by the river over hundreds of years. The train ran tight along its precipices and over several bridges, viaducts and tunnels; thrilling enough for both of us.

We were amused by the station in Pukarangi, a small building scarcely larger than the one Dad put his lawnmower in at home.

The rail cars were comfortable for their age and had open-air observation platforms if you like to look over the edge straight down with the wind in your hair. Thom took a turn or two but I opted to stay inside, like the chicken I am and enjoy the view in a tamer style through the windows. We ate in the onboard café and shared a kiwi meat pie and a cheese roll so we could each taste both.

There were scheduled stops along the route where we could disembark for a stretch and take pictures; at one place we got off and actually walked across a bridge in front of the train, kind of scary but we loved the view; I took a picture of the train as it crept along behind us.

We've made it back to Tunnel Beach several times since that first day when I photographed the sheep. We explored the tunnel which was carved out by a family in the 1870's for access to their own private beach. I imagine they'd be pretty upset to know how many residents and tourists use it now. We usually go at low tide and walk the narrow beach, but the rock formation above provides a good seat when the tide is high.

So many photos taken during our stay, but when a person comes this far you don't want to risk taking too few, I reason.

The Royal Albatross Centre reception building lies just ahead and Thom parks the car.

"I know nothing about the albatross except that they're rumored to be bad luck for fishermen," I tell him with a smile though I don't believe in 'bad luck'.

"You know more than I do." He helps me from the car and delivers a sweet kiss before we walk into the building.

We're on time for our scheduled visit and assigned a guide who walks with us to the observation rail.

"Wow, are you getting this on the camera?" Thom asks as we stand a little breathless at the look-out point. The scent of the ocean carries on the breeze and the grassy slopes between us and the rocky shoreline are full of nests, each with a single egg or a growing fledgling with parent standing by.

"I've set my camera for 'movie," I tell him, "don't want to miss any shots of these birds."

"The parents mate for life and take turns raising their young," our guide tells us. "One will fly out to eat then return with food for the fledgling and spell the other."

Just now a white bird larger than either of us was prepared for, flies close over us.

"Oh...my hands are shaking," I laugh, "good thing there's stabilization on this camera."

"Their wings are one of the largest wingspans of any bird, from three and a half metres and more," our guide continues. "They spend most of their life in the air and range thousands of miles from their nesting grounds."

We're surprised to learn that after the young birds learn to fly they don't return to earth in their first five years of life.

"When they do finally come in it's a bit of a bungle." The guide laughs as he explains, "Land is hard, water is soft, and they're used to landing on water so they usually crash-land on their first couple of tries."

"Is the albatross safe, I mean, are they endangered?" Thomas asks.

"Sadly, there are many species already gone," he answers. "They can live to the age of 40 or 50 years, but in the southern Pacific their most frequent cause of death is the lone line fishing method for tuna. The birds become entangled in the line when they attempt to 'steal' the fish for themselves.

"We've developed methods in the threatened species program to 'help' young, inexperienced birds and sometimes even remove eggs to hatch in brooders." We continue to watch and take pictures until our tour time is up.

As we leave, I pick up a pamphlet on Fort Taiaroa and I'm surprised it literally lies beneath us. One of several fortifications built by the British in 1886 to repel potential attacks by Tsarist Russia, the Fort holds the only working Armstrong Disappearing gun in the world.

The gun is unique in the way it operates; aimed while underground, it rises up to fire a six mm shell over 7300 meters then lowers itself by the power of its recoil. Not really one of my interests, but Thomas is disappointed we'll miss it today.

The lighthouse was built in 1864 and presently sits on a reserve at the tip of Taiaroa Point; the red roofs of the light and keeper's house are partially visible from the Albatross Center. It's been active for a hundred and forty-seven years and the Port Authority now maintains it. Though we're disappointed we won't get to see it up close we understand the need to protect it.

"What are you thinking my love?" Thom asks. He puts his arm around me to walk to the car as the sun begins its descent behind us.

"It's just...this trip couldn't have been any better. Being here with you where your family lived and worked has given me so much more understanding of what they experienced than I could ever imagine from books and papers.

"Then there's you and me," I turn to him, "I've become quite acclimated to you Mr. Smith and I hope I haven't been too tough on you in the process?"

"Not too tough, Mrs. Smith, but I do hope we'll continue to practice more after we get home." He plays with a strand of my hair that blows in the breeze.

"I look forward to it my darling," I answer.

Thomas leans on the terrace rail outside our room this morning. "There's something I'd like to do before we leave."

"That's day after tomorrow; do we have time?" I ask him.

"We should have...I want to see what's left of the old Arthur Street cemetery and lay wreaths; one for Rose and one for Catherine."

He's serious about it and I know our trip has made an impression on him.

"I'd love to help, dear."

We did find out, between the library and a very nice woman named Kay at the funeral service downtown, that Arthur Street was the first cemetery for settlers in the early 1800's. Many names aren't on its Memorial and I'd hoped there'd be a clue for Rose and Catherine's final resting places in James' journal. But both Harley and his wife told us they'd never found some of their forefathers. Many settlers' gravesites were lost, their markers eroded or removed.

"I don't think people placed as much importance at that time on formal graves," I remark. "They moved on and struggled to survive themselves."

"You're right," Thom agrees, "I read that cows and livestock had the run of the cemetery and graves weren't cared for until the city started pushing families to do so. I suppose there were many who didn't even have family here but it's hard to accept that some of those early settlers' resting places were lost."

"Thomas, though neither Rose nor Catherine are recorded on a list, we have to accept that your ancestor probably lies somewhere in the Arthur Street property given the approximate dates of their deaths." I take his hand and tell him tenderly, "You know she isn't there, don't you? Your grandmother's spirit has been flying free for years now and she's gone on."

"Yes, I know that," he answers, "but I like to think she'll somehow know who I am and be touched that I'm thinking of her."

"I believe she will my dear and we'll make the trip this afternoon."

Then I think of something else; "I have a proposal for tomorrow, too."

"Oh do you now?" He smiles at me and teases, "Why am I not surprised?"

"I don't know if you noticed Clark's Mill on the Heritage list?" I dig out the pamphlet from my bag and hand it to him.

"Heritage New Zealand...purchased Clarks Mill in 1977...labyrinth of early machinery...restored..." He looks up at me.

"It sounds like fun; are you sure you want to spend your last day in a mill though? After all, we're going home to one."

"Yes, I'm sure. You know how I feel about historical landmarks and I'd love to tour it with you. What do you think?"

"If you're sure about it Sarah, who am I to say 'no'? Besides, I'd love to see how the mill ran back in the day."

We find the granite, obelisk-style memorial in the old Arthur Street cemetery property on City Rise. It's visible from the busy intersection of Rattray, York Place and Arthur streets, in one of the oldest areas of the city.

Most of the previous cemetery land is now taken up by a high school and public park playground for children; rather appropriate since many of the children playing on the thick green grass just may be descended from these pioneers.

We walk from the car to read with respect the sixty names inscribed on its granite then place our two wreaths inside the low wrought-iron fence around its base.

With its position high above the city, the vista from the Park affords us a special view of Signal Hill, but typical urban sprawl partially hides what must have at one time been a spectacular view of the harbor.

We stand together taking it all in. "What's going through your mind dear?" I ask my husband.

"I'm trying to imagine what all this must have been like when Daniel and Rose came here in 1848, all these hills tree-covered and streams running free to the harbor. Hard to imagine now, isn't it?" he remarks as we look over the heavily populated scene.

"Natives probably worked from their fishing boats along the shore and there were only a few flimsy buildings on one main road up the hill from the dock; remember the museum's diorama of that period when we visited?"

"I do," Thom says, "and it must have been amazing for them, coming as they did from the U.K. where economics at the time were so depressed and seeing all this rich land before them."

"I can only think they were excited and thankful at the sight of it," Thom turns to me, "a second chance in a new country. In some way, I feel attached here, too."

"It's a big part of your roots dear;" I tell him, "one can always sense that."

"I suppose you're right Sarah. I don't know if we'll ever return, but I'm glad we've come. Thank-you for all this my love," he takes my hand and we stroll back to the car.

This morning we motor north toward old Clark's Mill; the weather is good and we hope it holds until our plane is away tomorrow afternoon.

"The directions say to look for the Maheno sign." I drive slower while Thom keeps a lookout.

This will make almost three weeks of driving on the left for me. I feel confident that when we return to Highbridge, I'll have no problem driving there. Funny how your brain can revise every driving habit you've formed since sixteen in only a few weeks.

"Here it is." Thomas points and I take the turn.

The Mill is an impressive three story high building with many windows. The water race is no longer active after conversion to electric power in the 20th century, but the Kakanui River runs nearby as if to keep an eye on its old warrior. We read in the library there's been serious flooding here in the past, being in the bend of the river as it is.

We've just made it by eleven a.m. and see a few people gathering for the tour. I follow Thomas who's practically jogging in his enthusiasm to join them. As for me, I'm enjoying the beauty of it all and appreciate that the Mill is still here after almost a hundred and fifty years.

Our tour guide shows us the old machinery first with its various drive arms, huge gears and belt system. When he starts it up it's very noisy and he laughs saying "always good to hear this sound, a sign it's working perfectly."

While Thom follows him upstairs, I linger to take in the patina of the walls that have seen so much history.

The Mill was built in 1865 from Omaru limestone block, some of which was taken from the hill behind it and some from a nearby quarry. In its day the water race brought power to the underhand wheel, the same type as ours at home, then returned the water to the River.

It can't be so much different here from our modern mill, can it? I envision the grain delivered as it was by oxen and draft horse in Daniel's time; not the fancy semi that pulls up to our double doors.

The grain was milled the same way by large round stones, slowly grinding until the fine flour stage was reached. I think of the grain dust by which many mills burned to the ground after a random spark set off an explosive inferno. The vacuum system at Copper Swift all but eliminates that risk.

Okay, mills have come a long way since this one was built, but I conclude it's good this mill still stands for history's sake and reminds us just how far we've come.

The upstairs windows offer me a glance outside through their small-paned sashes; potential frames for the view of the meadow that slopes away toward the river. Wild flowers have taken up residence and birds fly over to snap up insects that visit the blooms. I turn off my camera flash to take several shots through the glass panes and hope at least one will be worthy of framing for the wall in our own Mill.

I take more photos of the old grist stones someone thought to save when the mill converted to its modern roller system. *Their worn designs are much more romantic than modern steel rollers will ever be,* I think to myself.

"Sarah, there you are," Thom says from behind me. "I wondered what happened to you."

"Sorry, I got sidetracked with my photography. Are you finished with the tour already?" I ask and put my camera down.

"Yes, but it's been forty-five minutes you know." He smiles as he asks, "Did you enjoy your time here?"

"Actually I did; probably for different reasons than you. It's a lovely mill and I always feel others' history in venerable places like this. How was the tour?" I ask him.

"It was great; the gentleman who led us through is a retired miller born and raised here. He had some good stories and had us laughing.

"The Mill really contributed to Omaru's economy, even exported flour to Australia in the mid-19th century," Thom continues. "Apparently this area was quite prominent in wheat production and supported several mills which generated revenues comparable to sheep farming. This is the only working mill surviving today thanks to restoration by New Zealand's Historic Places Trust and people who volunteered to help restore it."

"I knew you'd be totally into this," I smile at him. "I have one or two photos to take and I'll be ready to go. Stand over there," I direct him, "I want one of you inside that doorway."

We're near our hotel when Thom remarks, "This is our last return to our home away from home and another great day wasn't it?"

"The entire trip has been tremendous, dear. You know, now that we're close to leaving I'm already getting homesick for Highbridge, though."

"Me too" Thom answers, "I can't wait to tell Dad what we've found and show everyone our pictures."

"It was fun taking them, but it'll be several weeks before I can get them in some sort of viewable order."

"We'll be patient." He leans over to give me a kiss.

Two days and four flights later, we have a real appreciation for our journey down to New Zealand with its many layovers and sightseeing in Florida and California.

On the return, we did it straight on with only hours between planes except from Sidney to Abu Dhabi where we almost slept through our fourteen hour layover, thank heaven for alarm clocks.

Seeing the car pull up with Berty and Stephen inside never looked so good.

"Stephen— it's so good to see you!" I call to him as he alights from the car in the pickup lane.

"How are you both?" He hugs us as Berty puts our luggage into the trunk. "You both look weary but healthy and a little suntanned."

"Yes, we're both fine, but exhausted from two days of flying and so glad to be home," I tell him as I sink into the back seat.

"It's sunny there Dad, hard to believe with this weather, I know," Thom tells him before joining me in the car.

Berty gets us out on the motorway in no time and even brought a few beverages along, knowing we might be parched after our travel.

The weather is directly opposite New Zealand's as expected and a cold rain falls lightly on the road ahead. The difference in temperature tells me we're really home again and I put my jacket on for the ride.

When we roll up to Highbridge Meg and Emily greet us at the door and we drag ourselves inside.

"Everything looks beautiful here Ems – we're so happy to be home," Thomas says.

"We're glad you're both safe and sound, sir," she declares. "It hasn't been the same around here without you two. Will you be staying the night or going to the cottage?"

I look at Thom, he looks at me and the same question is going through both our heads...*which would be easier?*

"I believe we'll be staying here tonight," he answers. "I don't think we have the energy for another car trip, even if it is short."

"Very good sir," she says and turns to Berty, "Please take their luggage up."

"How about a bowl of chicken soup and some crackers before you retire?" Stephen asks. "It always helped me after those dratted international flights I used to travel."

"You know, that sounds wonderful," I respond.

"Yes, it does," Thomas says. He takes my hand and Stephen follows us down to the kitchen where Jamie is already serving up his delicious brew.

"Jamie, I thought you'd be down at the Mill" I greet him with a hug and take a seat then lean over to inhale steam from the bowl he's brought to the table.

"How's it going at the Cafe?" Thom asks him.

"I switched for an hour with Chris; just wanted to see you both were in good shape. It's going well, Thom. We had a full house for dinner Saturday night and got some good feedback for the menu."

"That's great; glad to hear it. Good news always makes a great welcome home."

One hour later Thomas and I have showered and fade into sleep on the familiar bed in my old room at Highbridge.

Chapter Fifteen – The Shell

The pale green of the spring forest surrounds Highbridge and takes me by surprise as I drive in this morning. May feels early and I've barely noticed with all the excitement over the Mill and our trip to New Zealand.

Married life hasn't been all blissful moonlight and sunshine since we've been back. Thomas and I have had little time to savor our new married status since the honeymoon trip; marketing for the Mill has taken a sizeable portion of our time.

We did take a few hours last week to finally sit down with Stephen and Meg to show them the wealth of information on Daniel and his family we collected on our trip. They were amazed and thrilled at the flash drive containing James' journal and his connection with Daniel's friend and business partner Ethan. Meg has begun to read the journal and take notes.

As I open the front door this morning, I'm surprised to see Berty standing off to the side in the entry. It reminds me of another time, my first day here when his quiet disdain for my cat Tom was very clear.

He referred to Tom as the 'domestic' and asked where I wanted him placed. It was my first experience with a family 'inside man', as Thomas describes him and he sounded a little pretentious to my American ears.

I've come to know him better over the past year and now see beyond that facade of professional dignity. He's a very simple man, well-mannered and uncomplicated and has served this family well for a number of years since high school.

"Good morning Berty."

"Good morning, Mrs. Smith."

"I'll be in the library if anyone needs me," I tell him and start to walk on.

"Ms. Sarah, might I have a few moments of your time this morning?" I'm surprised since the last time we ventured into small talk was during the Christmas holidays.

"Of course Berty, what is it?"

261 | Copper Swift

"I'd prefer to discuss it in the Library if it isn't too inconvenient, mam, in confidence."

Berty checks his tie, picks up a pencil from the table and deposits it back into its container before he raises his eyes to me across the table.

"Ms. Sarah, this isn't easy for me to put into words, but while growing up in the village and during my employment, I've acquired some knowledge of this family's history."

I'm surprised at the subject he opens but remain attentive and allow him to continue.

"As a child I became intrigued with the idle talk of those around me; parents, relatives and others living in the area, specifically about hidden treasure here at Highbridge. When you discovered the secret library shelf last year it only served to make me more curious." He sits up straighter as if the chair is uncomfortable.

"I'd planned to speak about this earlier in the year, but with the Mill, the wedding preparations and holidays, it's taken me longer to do so." He stops and I wonder what in the world he's trying to say. Just as I'm about to ask, he continues.

"I've been secretly investigating the house and grounds for treasure throughout my employment." His words fall out so quickly they're almost connected to each other.

For a moment neither of us speaks. I'm totally shocked by his confession, certain I should not be the one here and Thomas or Stephen should be.

"Why are you telling me this Berty? The Smiths deserve to be told as your employers."

My natural curiosity takes over though and I have to ask, "What's your motivation to do this? Did you think to steal from them?"

He stands up, "No, absolutely not. I would never steal from them. This has been my home and family for decades. They've been fair and good people and I just want to pay them back by discovering any truth to the rumors."

I think he's being truthful, but wonder...*has he overheard bits about the Trust?*

"Berty, do you know about the Estate's finances?" He drops his eyes and silently sinks back to his chair.

"Yes mam, but not intentionally. Please know that I respect the family's privacy and would never skulk about to listen at corners nor do I discuss anything outside these walls. I overheard words on different occasions and now understand there's danger of the Estate's failure."

"Go on Berty." I wait to hear his side of this before I bring in Stephen and Thomas.

"I was devastated when I realised it was a possibility. You see Ms. Sarah I've always thought of this as my home, too. The searches had been a hobby, but then it became necessity that I do something to help the Smiths. I thought 'What if there's more to be found and it's valuable?' I decided to start a concentrated effort to find out."

"Very well Berty, it appears you're being honest with me, what is it you want?"

"Only your support to arrange a meeting with the family; I want to tell them myself so there's no question their concern is uppermost in all of this. You yourself have an appreciation for the Estate's history and I think you believe there are more secrets here, too."

He leans toward me, "I know more now...but I'd like to have everyone together before I reveal it." I choose my words carefully as he sits back in his chair again.

"Alright Berty, I'll ask Stephen, Thomas and Meg to meet with us today if possible. I'll keep an open mind because for some reason I believe you're telling the truth and yes, I've always thought other secrets might exist here."

"Thank-you Miss Sarah, your confidence in me is appreciated..." I interrupt him.

"That doesn't mean that Stephen and Thomas will feel the same and now that you've told me I must tell them, whether or not you go ahead with a meeting. You understand that don't you?"

"Yes, I do Miss Sarah and I accept the consequences, good or bad, but...," he hesitates, but says no more.

"Yes, Berty?"

"Nothing, beg your pardon mam, I'm done; thank-you for listening." He remains at the table while I leave to see Meg.

I happen to know that both Stephen and Thomas are at the Mill to review some details for the new apprentice program.

"Megs, could you please do me a favor and see if Stephen and Thom can spare an hour to come up here for a meeting?" She looks surprised but pulls up their calendars.

"They had an earlier meeting with Edward but should be done by now; I'll call them." She moves to pick up the phone.

"You need to be present as well Meg; the meeting is with Berty."

"Berty? What's this all about?"

"Surprisingly, it's about the Trust," I tell her. "I need to speak with you all before we see him in the library."

After briefing them on the subject we enter the library to find Berty at the window. He turns around and quickly returns to the table.

"Good morning Mr. Stephen, Mr. Thomas, Mrs. Smith. Thank-you for coming on short notice," Berty says.

"We had no choice, did we?" Stephen says solemnly and takes his seat.

"Berty, this is pretty serious," Thomas says. "You've admitted to Sarah you've been sneaking around under our noses, 'investigating' as you put it, the contents of our home. The fact that you see nothing wrong with that bothers me the most."

"I'm afraid I must agree with my son," Stephen adds, "However, at Sarah's request I'll let you have your say uninterrupted; only because I've come to value your services and think of you as part of this family at least up until now."

"I understand sir and after you hear me out I'm prepared to leave if that's your wish." Berty folds his hands on the table and proceeds.

"A month ago I began to hear scattered pieces of conversation about the possibility the Estate could be lost. It was by accident that I put the information together. I don't make a habit of invading anyone's privacy, especially yours. You've all been like family to me for a long time and I have only the highest respect for you.

"Ms. Sarah asked earlier what my intentions were and I told her truthfully that since childhood it's been a hobby to gather information on Highbridge anywhere it's available and I'd like to prove that to you." He reaches down to pick up a rather worn journal and lays it on the table.

"This is an account I've kept on Highbridge and the people who lived here since I was twelve years old. As a child I had opportunity to hear my elders talk; they thought I was too young to be interested, but it's all in here and accurate to the way it was told. I'd like to present it to you Ms. Sarah as a gift, no matter what you decide here today."

I accept the journal, the genealogist in me hopes it will provide some new information on Stephen's earlier family.

"I was the one who put the early letters from Regis to his father Angus in with those on your desk Mr. Stephen" Berty continues with his account, "and the one who found them under the front stairs in this tin box." He reaches again to the floor and brings a box to the table for us to see. It's rather battered by time and wear its dark green paint worn off here and there and the gold lines on its edges are faded.

"I take no pride in telling you all this. I know it created worry and that was unintended; especially for my superior, Miss Emily, whom I admire very much."

Stephen clears his throat, "Berty, we've heard enough."

"Yes, you must know that trust is paramount to our family Bert," Thomas adds, "and to hear that you've been invading our privacy with your midnight sorties is just more than you can ask us to condone and forgive."

"I think..." I begin slowly and clearly, "we have to pause on that path to see what else Berty has to say." I turn to him while Meg, Thomas and Stephen remain silent for the moment.

"Well Berty?" I ask.

"The fact is Ms. Sarah that a few weeks ago, I walked to the garden at Miss Emily's request to cut a few flowers. I needed a pair of snips and stopped in the greenhouse to retrieve the ones John keeps there then lingered to admire the fountain before leaving.

"Has anyone ever noticed the design under the fount?" He asks us. We look at each other in askance, *what is this man talking about?*

"For the sake of continuing, the answer is 'no' Berty, we've never noticed," I say a little impatient with him.

"Until you found the secret shelf Ms. Sarah and the brass letter seal I hadn't either; that's why I took notice. The design under the fount is the same shell sculpted in relief as the image in hollow-relief on the brass seal." He pauses a moment then gets to his point rather abruptly.

"You should take the brass seal to the greenhouse to see if it's useful there." He stops and I hear the hallway clock quietly tick-tock and the sound of John's men mowing the lawn outside.

Stephen finally speaks, "So you think there's some connection between the seal and the fountain?" He asks quietly, a rather blank look on his face.

"It's a possibility since the greenhouse was built at the same time as the house," Berty answers. "I don't know if you're aware, but it's been rumored for years in the village that part of the Smith fortune was hidden at the Estate when the house was built."

"That's just ridiculous," Thomas says and gets up from the table. "We have to talk among ourselves and decide what to do about all this. Please wait in the hallway Berty and we'll call you in when we're ready."

"Yes sir." Berty removes himself to the hall and closes the door quietly.

"Well," Stephen begins, "quite a tale, eh? I'm not sure how to take all this. On the one hand I want to believe him and on the other I feel I've been betrayed."

"I know what you mean dear," Meg says, "Berty's been someone I've trusted above all else, but now I don't know how to think about him. Just the fact that he's kept this secret for years makes me question his integrity."

"I've known Bert since childhood. Dad, you hired him when we came to Highbridge. He was always good to me as a child and never acted devious or unfaithful to the family that I know of. This is quite a shock, what do you think, Sarah?"

"I think two points need to take priority here; one, he came to us in honesty when he realised he may have found something to benefit us not himself."

"You believe he wasn't in it for personal gain," Stephen says.

"Yes, I do."

"Well then, what's your second point?" Thomas asks.

"More a question; can we all find it in ourselves to trust him again?" I ask. A silence falls for a few moments as we consider it.

"I don't think we'll know the answer until this plays out," Stephen says thoughtfully. "I'm going upstairs to get the seal. Meet me back here with Berty and we'll take a walk to the greenhouse."

John's men have finished mowing when we enter the yard from the kitchen door and the newly-cut grass sticks to our shoes as we walk across the garden.

"Good morning Ms. Sarah," John our head gardener says as I pass by and I hear him greet Stephen, Thomas, and Meg behind me. His crew watches with curiosity from the garden shed and we probably do present an unusual sight. They've never seen all of us take a walk together like this, led by Berty.

He leads us inside the greenhouse to the fountain and points to the shell design under the falling water.

"I've never noticed that," Thomas says in surprise, "I'll go out and turn the water off."

When the water stops, Stephen takes the seal from his pocket and compares its design to that on the fount. We all agree it's an exact copy in relief.

"Put the seal over the fount's design," I suggest, an idea that just came into my mind though I can't imagine why. Berty's eyes are fixed on mine and his face wears an odd expression I can't interpret.

"Better still," I tell Stephen, "give the seal to Berty. This is his idea so he should be the one to try it." Stephen looks surprised, but holds out the seal.

Berty proceeds to carefully fit it over the shell on the large center column of the fountain. It's a perfect fit and on a hunch he tries to turn the seal like a key, with no success. He looks up at us in doubt, but doesn't give up.

"Perhaps we should give it a tap to loosen it after these many years," he suggests. Thomas, by now encouraged retrieves a hammer from John's tool box and inflicts too good solid whacks on the end of the seal over the shell.

Berty tries again and this time the shell can be turned with considerable effort to the right. After a half turn renders it upside down we're stunned to see the hexagonal column of the fountain begin to move then shed six narrow panels of its granite.

We all step back, but each falls slowly, directly opposite of what one would expect for their weight. Like petals still attached to the base of some huge granite flower they continue and come to rest on the top edge of the fountain's basin. We stare in amazement at a hollow core inside the column and at what tumbles out.

Berty reaches to retrieve a white rock from the many that now lay in the fountain's bowl. He examines it inquisitively then hands it to Stephen who turns it over and over in his hand.

On a hunch, he withdraws a folding pocket knife from his trouser pocket and begins to scrape the surface of the rock several times with the blade. He pauses then looks up at us.

"I think it's gold," he says in a hushed voice.

We crowd around to see for ourselves, but I notice Berty hangs back.

"Berty do you want to see?" I invite, but he glances first at Stephen and Thomas to make sure. They motion him over and put the nugget back in his hand; a wide smile spreads over his face.

"My word," he declares and looks just as shocked as we are. We can't help but laugh at the look on his face and regain our voices again.

"What do we do now?" I ask.

Stephen, always the practical one suggests, "We take it to the house until we decide that, my dear. Thomas, get those buckets over there, we'll load them on the garden trolley."

Meg and I watch as the men move the gold to three buckets on the wagon.

"Where do we go from here Dad?" Thom asks as he makes ready to pull the wagon to the house.

"I believe a call to my banker for some guidance is in order my boy," Stephen says. "He'll know the procedure for handling gold deposits."

"First things first though; could you go out and give John and his crew the rest of the day off? Best to keep this as quiet as possible for now, don't you agree?" Stephen asks.

"Agreed, Dad, I'll go right now," Thom answers.

We wait in the greenhouse until he returns a short time later and prepare to leave for the house with the gold. Before we can do so, Berty walks again to the fountain.

"Mr. Thomas, could you please look at something here?" He points to the opening in the bottom of the fountain's bowl where the water pipes pass through.

"The opening is a little large for pipes don't you think?" Berty asks. "I tried to see down there past them, but it's too dark." A flashlight is quickly found and Thomas shines it into the hole then looks up in disbelief.

"I think Berty has something here." He hands the flashlight off to Stephen.

"There's more in there," Stephen reports, "but I don't know how we'd ever retrieve it."

"This fountain was built in several pieces Dad; maybe we just need to have someone disassemble it." I can tell Thom is struggling to keep control, but the smile on his face is contagious.

We can't help but share a hug then Stephen and Meg do the same. We're cautiously optimistic over the importance of the find, but know we should wait to celebrate until after the final recovery.

I look over to Berty who stands watching with a smile on his face. I realize he's the one we should be thanking and offer my hand to him.

"Berty, you have my gratitude for this; thank-you so much for pushing ahead."

"You are most welcome Ms. Sarah," he says, "I only hope it's enough."

"Whatever the amount it's more than we had before, so thank-you." I'm surprised as I turn around to find Thomas and Stephen waiting behind me to offer their thanks as well.

"Thank-you for your efforts Berty," Stephen says. "We'll still need to consider your behavior and I'd like you to take the next week off while we sort this out. I expect you to hold all in confidence during that time."

"Understood sir," Berty acknowledges and without further remark, leaves the greenhouse.

"Hard to do that in view of all this, but it had to be done," Stephen says.

"You're right, of course Dad." Thomas's face tells me a different story though and I have a feeling Berty can't be counted out just yet.

The family thanked me for my help and insight I think as I drive home, feeling odd to be doing so at this hour of the day.

I had to hold back and not admit that it was him; *that kindred spirit* who showed me the shell under the fount and brought me back to the compartment under the column when the others were ready to leave.

I know in my gut the spirit is someone from the Smith's past and they should know that he cared so much he was willing to cross again into this world to take care of his own.

If I only knew who he is or rather, was I could at least tell Ms. Sarah. *Maybe one day in the future I'll be able to do that* I think hopefully.

For now it's a good feeling to know I've been able to contribute, no matter what the outcome on my job.

I'll take the week off, catch up on some chores at home then think about possible work I might pursue, should my job status change.

Deep down I feel good about all of it, except the scare I gave Miss Emily. She's come to mean more to me over the years and I would never harm her in any way.

Otherwise I'm proud of the job I've done for the family...with no regret.

Stephen said yesterday, "Sarah, a 'new normal' is taking shape for all of us thanks to Berty." I've taken it to mean he's considering leniency on Berty's behalf.

The whole event continues to replay in my head during my daily drives to Highbridge. It's surreal to remember the gold spilling from the old fountain and the surprise on everyone's faces, including Berty's. The fact that I witnessed the discovery of a family's heritage is something I couldn't have foreseen in a million years.

I feel that none of us has returned to our 'normal' lives nor will we ever be the same, as Stephen so wisely said.

Trusted staff and heavy equipment were utilized last week to disassemble the granite fountain and move it off its base. Below, we found more gold; over five-hundred kilos in nuggets lay in the granite-lined space.

Stephen and Thomas oversaw the gold's removal and arranged for its storage and security off the Estate until it can be assayed and valued. Decisions are being made on investment options after final value is determined and an investments professional has been hired to manage the Estate's Trust.

We voted to rebuild the fountain on its original granite foundation in the greenhouse, exactly as it was placed by Angus so long ago.

Meg and I will soon oversee a 'spruce up' of the old greenhouse with a new area for social gatherings, perhaps to let for weddings. We love the idea and think it would be breathtaking with a few chandeliers and of course some auxiliary heat for our chilly weather. Even the men were on board when we brought up the idea and they left it in our hands to make it happen.

Our 'women's alliance' between Meg and I seems to be working and we have other plans to generate revenue and save money for the Estate. We know patience will be needed and the men won't be expected to adjust too rapidly to any new plans, especially in Stephen's case.

There's a chance the media will eventually visit and Stephen has prepared a statement though we expect when it does happen we will have our hands full for a while until the story dies down.

Thom suggested we go ahead and announce the event which would give us better control. He and I both have ideas about adding it to the Estate's lore; after all, we do have the Copper Swift Mill and Jamie's' Café to promote now. Stephen is against the use of what he feels is a 'private family matter' for commercial incentive and we agree to put away our suggestions for now, in consideration of his wishes.

Stephen, Meg, and Thomas are in the kitchen as I walk in this morning and I hear Stephen say, "How did they think their plan for the gold would be passed down?"

"I think I may have the answer to that," I tell him as I hang up my jacket by the door and come to the table where Chef Chris has already served breakfast.

"I reread the last two letters from Regis to Angus this morning and I'd like you take another look at the last one." I hand a copy to each of them.

"Regis prepares his father for his possible demise in India by writing this letter," I explain. "He mentions 'passing the shell to Charles' and 'explaining what must be done in future to preserve and protect it.'

"For some reason, either Angus didn't have a chance to talk with Charles or perhaps Charles was unable to speak with you Stephen. Either way it's obvious that up to that time the gold's secret was passed down the line of your family patriarchs by word of mouth. When that broke down the next generation didn't receive the information."

"You may be right Sarah," Stephen says, "there's another aspect to all this." He pauses as if searching for the right words.

"I thought about my father's role in this all night long and something came back to me." He drops his eyes to his hands and clasps them together on the table.

"Charles asked for me in his last hours...but I was stuck in London at the damned Company and couldn't get home before he passed." He stops, his head low in silence as Meg reaches for his hand, but after a moment he continues.

"That may have been the crucial point when word of mouth failed and why I knew nothing of this. It's clear to me that our family's legacy would have remained a secret until the fountain was dismantled."

Meg pats his hand, "Now dear there was no way you could have reached him from London before he passed. Everything has worked out hasn't it? Be satisfied that it has my dear."

Thomas comes to lay his hand on Stephen's shoulder, "It's all water under the bridge Dad, no regrets, okay?" Stephen puts his hand over Thomas'.

"Obviously the gold was meant to be protected over the years for future generations," Thomas says. "I'd really like to know more about how it was brought here and by whom. Was it by Daniel's efforts or those of his children?"

"We may never know that," I tell him, "but I'll be sifting through old documentation and James's journal for any clues." I bring out photos in an effort to ease Stephen's sadness.

"I took pictures of our discovery event and you guys look as if you're archeologists digging up historic relics." I kid them and pass the pictures around.

"Well, my back certainly felt it," Thomas looks wistfully at me, "but I'm glad you took these. Our grandchildren will get a kick out of them someday."

"All this has certainly influenced my thoughts on Berty's activities," Stephen admits.

Stephen, Thomas, Meg and I meet this morning to make a decision on Berty's continued employment. It's ten days now since his discovery and he was asked not to mention the treasure to anyone in that time.

"We have to give credit where it's due" I say. "Berty's lengthy hobby is what led to this discovery and nothing else."

"You're right Sarah and Dad's correct, the gold would have stayed there for the millennium," Thomas laughs. "Our ancestor certainly had a sense for good hiding places.

"And I'd just like to add, I believe that based on what we know and with the discovery of the letters, Angus Smith built this house and probably had a hand in designing the fountain," Thom says. "It was quite ingenious with its water hydraulics which permitted those granite panels to slowly unfold. I'm just grateful he didn't design them after the Egyptians, who would have favored crushing any who discovered the treasure."

Everyone laughs and Stephen asks "Have you had a chance to glance through Berty's journal yet, Sarah?"

"Just briefly; I did see a reference to an elderly relative who visited from St. Thomas so I'll be following it up since it matches a remark from Em and may give us more on Briana Smith Gordon.

"Berty's given us an amazing account of hearsay that circulated through the village from the time the house was built. I like the information on families who actually worked here and honestly, so much has come out of this that I'll be kept busy for years."

"At first I felt betrayed by Mr. Berty," Meg speaks up, "until all of this was discussed. Now it appears he's actually performed a service for us without being asked to. I venture to say that, had he asked, would we have given him permission? Therefore, I say thank goodness he took it upon himself to go ahead. He's greatly contributed to the Estate's wellbeing and preserved history that would otherwise have been lost."

"Thank you my dear," Stephen takes over our meeting, "Well said which brings us to a vote; those in favor of retaining Berty on staff?"

We all say 'Aye'.

"If you'll humor me for one more topic," Stephen adds, "I've been thinking perhaps Berty should receive a finder's fee. He's given us a gift otherwise unavailable and since the value of the gold is estimated to be over the top, given today's price at £1800 per troy ounce, a 1% fee would equal roughly £281,000. Of course he'd pay tax on it or could defer that by investing. What do you think?"

Stephen calls Berty into the library where he checks the collar of his shirt before sitting down at the table with us.

"Well Berty, this has been a long ten days for everyone, especially for you I imagine?"

"Yes sir," He answers quietly.

"We've taken a vote on your continued employment and all voted 'yes', Stephen announces.

Berty rises saying, "Thank-you sir, very much."

"You're welcome Berty, but please, there's more to tell" and he motions him to sit down again.

"We've also decided that a finder's fee should be yours as a reward for uncovering the treasure and helping to assure the Estate's longevity into the future." Stephen leaves his chair and walks around the table to Berty.

"So it's with pride that I present this check to you in the amount of two-hundred and eighty thousand pounds." We all applaud and congratulate him.

"I...d...don't know what to say," Berty stutters. "This is too generous of you all, are you sure?" he asks in disbelief.

"Yes, we're sure Berty," Stephen tells him. "Your 'hobby' and natural curiosity have greatly contributed to the Estate and to our knowledge of my family's history. We're very grateful and your job waits for you, should you desire to continue."

"Yes, we ask just one thing only," Thomas adds. "If you wish to conduct further searches in the house or grounds, work with Sarah and clear it first. We would prefer to have it all above board and during the day so there's no summoning the Constable for unusual sounds in the night," he finishes solemnly and then breaks into a smile.

"Oh yes sir, fully understood and I vow there will be no more nighttime expeditions," Berty promises.

"Good," Stephen says as he shakes Berty's hand then gives him a business card.

"If you need help with how to handle your finder's fee Berty, here's my banker's number. It might be a good idea to let him help you regarding taxes and what to do next, that sort of thing."

"Thank-you very much sir and thank-you, all," he tells us then leaves to report to Emily.

"That was fun," I say. "I've never given away that much money, did you see the look on his face?"

"Yes and it was well deserved, Sarah," Stephen adds. "I imagine it will be a nest egg for his retirement in another ten or fifteen years; gratifying to see he doesn't have a big head over it all."

"Do you think Berty will stay?" Thomas asks, "He has funds now, maybe he'll want to break loose in life a little; he's served others since high school."

"Well, we couldn't blame him, could we?" Meg says, "It's not everyday something like this happens."

"No, we couldn't and if he did leave, I'd have nothing but good wishes for him; he deserves it," Thomas adds.

"Here, Here," Stephen says.

"Well, is there something else Berty?" I ask a little shortly as he holds me up from my morning rounds.

"There is Miss Emily, but I'm having a hard time finding the words."

Berty has been back to work for several weeks now and I must say; it's good he's returned.

"Well then just start as I haven't all day to dally here," I tell him.

He responds quickly, "Yes mam. It's about the past events and concerning my behavior. I wish to apologize to you Miss Emily for the way I upset you with the coat closet incident."

"Nearly did me in Berty with that bit of farce."

"I realised my mistake too late Miss and want you to know how deeply sorry I am for the whole thing. I'd like to make it up in some small way with a gift for you and hope you'll accept this as a peace offering."

He pulls a small package out of his pocket and offers it to me. When I remove the lid, there's a pair of ear studs, gold with clear sets in them.

"Berty, these are lovely, I don't know what to say." I fumble in embarrassment for more words but really am at a loss.

"They're real diamonds Miss Emily to signify my heartfelt apology and my regard for you. I hope we can continue to work together as we have since there's nowhere else I'd rather be."

"That's very nice of you Berty and yes, I've already forgiven you because of the way you've helped the Smiths. Mr. Stephen told me all about it and I assured him it would go no further from me. He asked if I felt I could continue to work with you and I said that I could."

"You did?" Berty asks.

"Yes, I told him you were trustworthy, perhaps a little impulsive, but that you'd always been honest in your work here at Highbridge."

"Thank-you Miss Emily, that does my heart good." He stands looking at me and says no more so I take the initiative.

"Alright Mr. Berty if that's all, thank-you very much for the gift and let's get back to it, shall we?" I say rather abruptly.

"Yes mam," he answers as he turns away toward the front door.

I take one more look inside the box after he's gone then close it up and stuff it into my apron pocket. I retrieve a paper hanky at the same time and give my nose a wipe.

That was awfully nice of Mr. Berty.

Chapter Sixteen – The Last Secrets

G ood morning mam." Berty meets me at the front door to help with the empty stroller and baby tote. I put little Vail back into his seat; his blue eyes and dark hair make me fall in love all over again each time he looks at me; our little miracle baby and his father are both so precious to me.

"Thank-you Berty, he's becoming quite heavy and eating like an athlete. How are you this morning?"

He picks up the baby's bag to follow me down the hallway.

"Splendid mam, I finished six months on Mr. James' journal last night, quite fascinating his story is and I'm enjoying it immensely. I'm keeping a catalog of important facts on my laptop with page numbers and brief notes, just as you instructed."

"That's good and I can't wait to review some of it, but right now I need to get the baby to his grandmother Megs. Can you meet me in the library in say, thirty minutes?" I ask him.

"Yes mam, I've already checked with Miss Emily and she's freed the morning up for me here."

"Good, see you then." I push the stroller on through the hall and into the great room.

"Ah, there's my little lad," Megs exclaims and comes to pick up her grandson who breaks into his best adorable smile. I look at the two of them together and once again count my blessings.

Vail Stephen Smith arrived two months earlier than predicted. When Thom and I saw him so small and fragile it took everything we had to stay positive. But sure enough, he grew stronger each day until the doctors at last cleared him for discharge home. He weighed only four pounds then, but over the past five months he and his appetite have flourished.

"I'm meeting with Berty on the journal this morning," I tell Megs, "then Thom and I plan to take a walk about the Estate this afternoon. It's been a while since we've been off together or even had the energy for it!" I laugh.

"Now, I put plenty of extra formula, diapers, and food, including snacks, in this bag." I try to think of anything I've forgotten and can't.

"I think that's it Megs, can you think of anything?"

"Oh go on Sarah and have a pleasant afternoon," she declares with a smile. "You know once Stephen gets his hands on Vail, you won't get him back anytime soon." We laugh together knowing Stephen loves to carry Vail about and talk to him as they tour the house.

"You're right Megs, see you later," I tell her and return to the library where I take a seat at the window and wait for Berty.

After Vail's arrival home from the hospital it became clear just how much time a baby requires and left a lot less time to spend on Stephen's history and my own clients. I needed an assistant, someone interested in genealogy and above all, a self-starter I wouldn't have to continually stand over. I immediately thought of Berty; after all, his hobby was family research for years and he did it well.

When asked to help, he was thrilled to be considered and started as soon as we worked out his time and duties at the house with Stephen, Meg and Emily. He splits his time between Highbridge and my assignments and is very thorough in his work.

My right hand for three months now, I don't know how I made it through that first month without Berty's help. He's even made time for an online course in genealogy and I expect he'll continue his natural talent in the subject as a second career someday.

"Ms. Sarah, are you ready to meet?" Berty asks from the doorway.

"Yes, come in."

"There's something I'd like to share with you before we begin..." he says, his manner has changed to one of seriousness.

"What is it Berty, everything okay?"

"Oh yes mam. All is more than fine with me these days, thanks to you and Mr. Stephen. I just have something I've wanted to share with you since last year in my 'secret investigation' days and haven't found the right words to keep me from sounding like a raving looney."

He's apparently a little embarrassed by whatever it is and he's never used the slang 'looney' ever, I think.

"Well in that case Bert I've found the best method is to just get it out there and '*let the chips fall where they may*', as my Dad says."

"Very well mam, here it is. During my night time tours of Highbridge last year and in the greenhouse, I was witness to what I call a 'kindred spirit'. He appeared four times to me in the year; in three of those he actually guided me to the tin box, the shell on the fountain and to the gold under the fountain." He stops and I look at him dumbfounded.

"Berty, are you okay?" I finally ask, struggling to be realistic, but objective and finding the latter very difficult to achieve.

"Perfectly, mam," he says with cold logic as he stands quite steady.

"Good...because I never expected to hear anything like that from you."

"Yes mam," he says.

"Okay, the chips are down now, so why don't you sit with me and tell me more." I'm not sure what I'll hear next but try to remain open-minded.

"I encountered 'him' the first time as he stood by the mantel in the great room," Berty tells me. "The room was dark except for the low fire and it was only for a moment; on second glance, he wasn't there and I chalked it up to a reflection off the mirrors in the room."

"Very wise, Bert, I probably would have, too," I encourage him but ask myself, *what are you saying? You know you would have run like the coward you are.*

"Yes mam. The second time was more of a surprise. He appeared inside the hallway closet and stood in a fog of sorts by his own light. I thought at first the light came from my flashlight, but then noticed I'd never turned it on."

"Getting a little more serious now, go on." I direct him.

"The third appearance was again in the closet, but he pointed to the back of the stairs where I found the tin box. At that point I promised myself to take a closer look at him rather than back away as I'd been doing."

"That was very brave of you; what happened next?" I ask.

"His face appeared to me in the flow of water from the fountain then disappeared, leaving a clear view of the shell underneath the fount.

"The last event was the day the gold was found. Do you remember when I asked Mr. Thomas to come look again at the bottom of the fountain?" Bert asks then continues.

"I heard the spirit inside me telling me to do that."

"Bert, you understand I am a little disbelieving here, right?"

He nods, "Yes mam."

"Good...that's good," I trip a little. "Now I do have some questions and I guess my first is what did this 'spirit' look like?"

"His clothes were rather late eighteen hundreds, a waistcoat and a suit. He had a pleasant smile...and while in the coat room I noticed an obvious scar on his left forehead." Berty points to his own forehead to demonstrate.

My breath stops for a moment as I recall Harley Ferguson sitting at his kitchen table telling Thom and me about Daniel being shot. At first I reject it and rise from my chair to walk it off.

"Mam," Berty says, "Are you alright?"

The walking does no good though because in addition, I believe I may have experienced some of the same effects while in the greenhouse.

"Berty, this 'telling you', what was it like?" I ask.

"It wasn't words exactly just a sudden need to call Mr. Thomas over to look down the opening in the fountain. For some reason I did it without question, the direction was that clear in my mind," he finishes calmly.

Then it dawns on me, *it's the glance Berty gave me in the greenhouse before he called Thom over to the fountain.* He looked to me at the same moment the ghost was 'speaking' to both of us and his description is accurate. There was no voice yet our visitor's instructions were clear inside my head...and I think the spirit's identity is clear now, too.

"Berty, thank-you for telling me all this and I have something to tell you, too. I have reason to believe your friendly spirit was a manifestation of Daniel Smith. You'll understand how I know this when you come to his story in James' journal. Understand that I've never believed in 'spirits' here on earth before, but in this case I may have to make an exception." I smile at him and he meets it with a smile of his own.

"Perhaps this is a lesson to show that I don't know everything?" I tell him.

"Thank-you Ms. Sarah, it's a great relief to know that I'm somewhat in my right mind."

"You're very much in your right mind Berty, now let's get going on those notes of yours. I have an appointment at three o'clock that won't wait."

Thomas and I climb the hill behind Highbridge all the way to the upper fence line at the forest. The view of the countryside, the manor house and the Mill is most grand from up here. The late afternoon is a little cool with fall well underway; its colors sprinkled over the landscape in front of us set off the Copper Swift's dark flow on its way south.

"Whew" Thom takes a deep breath as we finally lean on the wooden fence. "It's been a while since I climbed that path, but I needed the exercise; how about you, darling?"

"Well I get all the exercise I need with little Vail, but just being here with you feels great. We've missed a lot of time together this year with all that's gone on and the baby's arrival; this is wonderful." His arm encircles my shoulders and we stand together taking in the late afternoon sun.

"You know Sarah; I made all my most important decisions in life right here where we stand."

"Really, I didn't know that dear; like what?" I ask him.

"Like whether or not to date a certain village girl during secondary school."

"Yes, that would be a heavy decision; do go on." I raise an eyebrow and look back at the western sky.

"Seriously," he continues, but I note he's hard-pressed to keep a straight face.

"I watched the Swift's flow from here and decided leaving Smith Imports was the right move. I also decided to marry you, my dear. Both decisions have been on target and at each one I thought '*Copper Swift has been moving all these years, I can move forward, too*'.

"Oh and did the Copper tell you it would take so long for me to marry you?" I kid him.

"No hint on that," he answers with a smile.

"You know, I envy you a bit Thom."

"How so?" he asks.

"You have so much history to build on; all palpable right here on this Estate to remind you your forefathers planned ahead for future generations. And our little Vail is next in line to share what they began."

"I am a lucky man," he agrees. I look up to meet his eyes and we share a tender kiss before I lay my head on his shoulder.

Then I tell him about his grandfather's recent visits. I'm a little surprised when I finish the tale he stands silent with no comment and watches the sun's descent.

"Thom?" He returns from wherever he's gone and looks at me with an awkward smile.

"Sarah, I wasn't ever going to mention it, but since you brought it up...my grandfather was 'with' me that day, too. I recognised him from Harley's description of the scar, okay?" He sees that I'm ready to protest his silence on the subject and continues to explain himself.

"I just thought it's not the sort of thing I'd describe openly to anyone and would do better to keep it to myself," he says and answers my unspoken question.

"If Berty hadn't the courage to describe it...," I confess to him, "who knows if I ever would have. We almost missed a chance to share an amazing experience together, didn't we?"

"Yes, that's true; from here on out, let's not do that anymore," he looks at me. "We need to be open with each other, no matter how silly or even bizarre the subject. I think we can trust each other to share thoughts...even if we agree to disagree?"

"I believe it now that we've shared the most far-fetched story we'll probably ever have," I laugh.

"Can you forgive me for not telling you sooner?" Thom asks.

If ever there were puppy dog eyes he has it down to a science and assures me I'm totally, undeniably in love with this man.

"Of course, if you can forgive me the same," I reply.

"Always my Sarah...always."

The sun is on the rim of the world by the time we finish our confessions and vows. Below us the Swift has become a living flow of coppery color under the day's last light.

We walk the twilight pathway back down the hill together and I wonder; who saw the Copper Swift this way long ago and named it so aptly?

End

Hope you've enjoyed reading
Copper Swift-Back to Highbridge
as much I've enjoyed writing the entire
Windows Trilogy.

Please leave a brief review at Amazon.com
Or a simple star rating.
Your time is greatly appreciated
Thank-you so much!

www.lindajpiferauthor.com
Amazon.com
Goodreads.com
Facebook.com/lindajpifer/
Pinterest